# RETURN TO THE ISLAND

KAY CORRELL

ROSE QUARTZ PRESS

Published by Rose Quartz Press

040218

*This book is dedicated to my manager. The person who keeps me on track, checks in on me, supports me, encourages me, and yells at me.*
*I love you.*

KAY'S BOOKS

Find more information on all my books at
*kaycorrell.com*

## COMFORT CROSSING ~ THE SERIES

The Shop on Main - Book One
The Memory Box - Book Two
The Christmas Cottage - A Holiday Novella
(Book 2.5)
The Letter - Book Three
The Christmas Scarf - A Holiday Novella
(Book 3.5)
The Magnolia Cafe - Book Four
The Unexpected Wedding - Book Five

The Wedding in the Grove - (a crossover short story

between series - with Josephine and Paul from The Letter.)

**LIGHTHOUSE POINT ~ THE SERIES**
Wish Upon a Shell - Book One
Wedding on the Beach - Book Two
Love at the Lighthouse - Book Three
Cottage near the Point - Book Four
Return to the Island - Book Five

**INDIGO BAY** ~ A multi-author sweet romance series
Sweet Sunrise - Book Three
Sweet Holiday Memories - A short holiday story
Sweet Starlight - Book Nine

Sign up for my newsletter at my website *kaycorrell.com* to make sure you don't miss any new releases or sales.

CHAPTER 1

Tally ambled along the beach near Lighthouse Point. A light spring breeze rustled her hair and tugged at the loose, oversized shirt she was wearing. She loved it when she had time to escape from Magic Cafe and have a few minutes to herself. Oh, she enjoyed owning Magic Cafe, but still, a few moments' peace was a welcomed blessing.

She paused to watch a handful of pelicans swoop by along the shoreline. The waves gently rolled to the shore today in the calm gulf water. How could the ocean look so serene at times when she knew just how angry and greedy it could get?

She scuffed some sand with her bare foot. The wind caught the grains and tossed them down the beach. She looked out at the sea, far out to the horizon.

This darn ocean.

If only she didn't love it so much because she hated it so.

She scrubbed her hands over her face, blocking the view, then opened her eyes and headed slowly back toward the cafe.

Billowing smoke caught her eye in the distance, and she picked up her pace to a measured jog. Her heart beat jaggedly from either the quickened pace or worry. As she got closer, she realized the smoke was coming from Belle Island Inn and her pulse raced.

Susan. Was her friend Susan okay?

Tally wasn't much of a runner, but she doubled her pace and rushed toward the inn, grabbing ragged breaths of air as she sped across the sand.

The island's fire truck jutted out on the side parking lot. A handful of firemen stood talking, but no one looked frantic. *That was good news, right?*

She spotted Susan standing on the beach and hurried up to her, bending over when she reached her friend to catch her breath. "Susan…" Tally sucked in some air. "Are you okay? What happened?"

A large streak of soot crossed Susan's face, and

her eyes were rimmed in red. "I'm okay. Everyone's okay."

"What happened?"

"Grease fire. It got out of control."

"Is there a lot of damage?" Tally scanned the building.

"Smoke damage in the kitchen and dining room. Water damage from the sprinkler system in the dining room. It's all such a mess."

"I'm so sorry." Tally put an arm around her friend. "At least you're okay."

Susan coughed. "It could have been worse. The fire chief said we'll have to close the kitchen, of course, and the dining room. But only a few rooms near the dining room had damage, so at least we can keep the inn open."

"You sure you're okay?" Tally eyed her.

"Yes, really I am."

"I think you should let the doctor take a look."

"Really, I'm fine." Susan coughed repeatedly.

"That's it. I'm taking you to the clinic to get checked out. Don't argue with me."

"But…"

"Mom!" Jamie, Susan's son, called out as he came racing up to them. "Are you okay?"

"I'm fine, dear. Really, I am."

Jamie wrapped his mother in a quick hug.

"No, she's not. She's coughing from the smoke." Tally glared at her friend.

Jamie released his mother and took a step back. He stood in front of her and eyed her from head to toe as if convincing himself she was okay. "I was at The Lucky Duck with Harry when I heard. You almost scared me to death. Couldn't get here fast enough. What happened?"

"Fire on the grill. It got out of control." Tally answered for her friend to save her from launching into another coughing fit. "Now, persuade your mother to let me take her to the clinic to get checked out."

"I'm fine."

"She'll go." Jamie's words were tinged in a no-nonsense tone.

Susan sighed. "Okay, okay." Then her eyes opened wide. "Oh, no."

"What?" Tally and Jamie said in unison.

"It's ruined."

"What's ruined? Mom, we can fix any damage to the inn. The important thing is you're okay. We'll work out the rest of it."

"No, not that. I know we'll get it repaired. That's not the inn that's ruined."

Tally tilted her head. "So, what's the big 'oh no' all about?"

"Julie."

"Julie was inside?" Jamie swiveled to stare at the inn.

"No. Not that."

"If you could help us out by not making us play twenty questions, I could get you to the clinic sooner." Tally crossed her arms.

"It's Julie's wedding. I've *ruined* it."

Tally and Susan joined Julie at The Sweet Shoppe for a late breakfast the next day.

"I told you we should have just eloped." Julie stared glumly into her coffee cup. "Or maybe we could just postpone it by a month or two."

"I'm sure Reed would just be thrilled." Tally rolled her eyes.

Julie didn't miss her friend's sarcastic tone. "But where am I going to find a place at this late notice?"

"I'm so sorry." Susan leaned back in her chair. "The timing is horrible. I just wish… I'm sorry."

"It's not like it's your fault." Julie fiddled with the spoon resting beside her cup. "I'm just glad that no one was hurt. I'm glad *you're* okay."

"Did you talk to your insurance guy?" Tally looked at Susan.

"I did. It should be covered. We'd been planning on upgrading things in the kitchen anyway and had funds set aside for that. So, I guess we'll do that now."

Julie couldn't believe that after she'd finally picked a date, picked a venue, and even found the perfect wedding dress, that everything had gone up in smoke. Literally. She immediately felt selfish for her thoughts. Susan could have been hurt, and now she had all the rehab to deal with on her inn.

"So have you had two cups of coffee?" Tally questioned her.

"What?" Julie glanced down at her t-shirt. "Oh." She had a slight addiction to t-shirts with sayings on them. Today's shirt proclaimed that 'everything looks brighter—right after the second cup of coffee.'

She shrugged. "It's actually like my fourth cup."

"Good. Things will look brighter. We'll have your wedding at Magic Cafe, of course. I'll close the restaurant for the evening. We'll set up chairs on the beach for the ceremony. It will be fine."

"I can't have you closing the restaurant for a whole evening." Julie frowned. "Though, Reed would probably insist on paying you for your lost income."

"Nonsense." Tally shook her head. "He will not. And I think this is a perfect solution."

"You could borrow the chairs from the inn." Susan nodded. "This could work. We'll figure out something for the arbor."

"I don't know what to say. Are you sure, Tally?" Relief started to seep through Julie. Magic Cafe would be the perfect substitute for the inn. It seemed fitting to have her wedding there since that's where she first lived and worked when she came to the island.

"I'm sure. We'll rent some tablecloths for the tables. Have the flower delivery moved to Magic Cafe." Tally frowned. "I don't really have a good room for you to use to get ready in except my office... and that's a crowded mess."

"Well, that's the least of my worries. I'm just happy to have a place to have the wedding. We have so many people coming. Reed knows a lot of people. It's going to be a lopsided wedding, though. You guys are my friends. That's about all who will be sitting on my side."

"How about Dorothy, Mary, Jamie, Cindy, Harry, and Sammy..." Tally rattled off more names.

Julie sighed. "I know. I'm just nervous about it. Reed has all these fancy friends coming from

Seattle. Business people. I'm just… well, I wonder what they'll think of me."

Tally shrugged. "Do you really care what they think?"

"I just want Reed to be proud of me. I want him to have the type of wedding he wants, too. I…" Julie pushed back her hair and at the same moment panicked. What was she going to do with her hair at the wedding? She hadn't even thought that through. She must be missing the basic female gene that made a woman know how to plan her own wedding, much less *want* to plan her wedding. She wanted to be married to Reed, but she'd just as soon have the wedding behind her. She had never liked being the center of attention.

"You deserve this. You do. Quit second-guessing yourself. You're going to have a beautiful wedding. Susan and I will make sure of it." Tally reached over and covered her hand. "Now, tell me why you just had that panicked look on your face. We'll fix it, too."

Her friend knew her so well.

CHAPTER 2

The next day, Tally tugged on the door to the storage building next to Magic Cafe. She wanted to make sure they had enough napkins for the wedding reception. Cloth napkins, of course. She couldn't abide by paper napkins at her restaurant even if more than half the tables were outside.

The door fought back, so she messed with it, gave it a hip check, and yanked on it yet again. Light poured into the main room as the door swung open. Just like in the story Goldilocks, she'd swear someone had been sleeping in the bed in the corner of the room. But no one had stayed here for years. Not since Julie had moved out. But the blanket was rumpled, and an opened can of nuts sat beside the bed.

Tally whirled around at the sound of movement in the corner. "Who's there?" She peered into the dark corner, then reached for the light switch and flipped it on, illuminating the far side of the room. "Come out or I'll call the sheriff."

"No. Please." A young woman stepped out of the shadows. "I'm sorry. I didn't mean any harm."

Tally scowled. "What are you doing here?"

"I…" The young woman looked at the door and Tally thought the woman might bolt for it, but instead, she stayed put. "I needed a place to stay last night. My car broke down. I… was going to just stay on the beach, or sleep in the car, but it got colder than I thought it would. I came in here and found the bed. I'm sorry. I'll pay you back for the container of nuts." The girl reached into her pocket and took out a handful of crumpled bills.

Tally eyed the girl. "Did you consider a motel? There are a lot of them on the island…"

"No, I didn't… I don't… have enough money for that."

"You just passing through?" Tally swept her glance from the top of the girl's mussed, just-woke-up hair to her worn tennis shoes with the side slightly split out.

"I was going to look for a job here, actually. Stay for a bit." The girl shifted from foot to foot.

Tally would guess the girl—young woman—was young to mid-twenties. She had a tinge of a haunted look in her eyes that tugged at Tally's heart. Tally let out a long breath.

"What kind of job are you looking for?"

"Anything. I'm a hard worker. I just need to earn some money."

"I don't suppose you know how to waitress?"

"I do." The girl said it a little too eagerly. Tally wondered just how experienced she actually was.

"Well, you're in luck. I need another waitress at Magic Cafe. Can you start today?" She figured the girl could use all the help she could get, and Tally knew what it was like to hit upon tough times.

"I... well, I could... but..." The girl swept her hand through her shoulder-length brown hair, sending it cascading away from her face.

"Well, what is it? Do you want the job or not?"

"I'd have to find something to do with..."

"Momma?" A small voice came from behind a box in the corner.

"Come on out, Bobby. It's okay."

A young boy slipped out from behind the box and came to stand beside the young woman.

KAY CORRELL

The woman set her hands on the boy's shoulders. "This is my son, Bobby."

Tally swallowed. All she'd wanted was the box of napkins. She was willing to give the girl a job to help her out… but now things were getting complicated. She figured the girl was raising Bobby alone, and she knew exactly how hard that was.

Tally sighed. "How about you two come over to the cafe and have a nice hot breakfast? We'll see what we can figure out."

"But I don't…"

Tally held up her hand. "On me. Call it my welcome to the island."

"Do you have pancakes?" Bobby's eyes lit up. "I haven't had pancakes in forever."

"We do."

The boy grinned and Tally stared at him. Then she swallowed and brushed her hand over her face. The boy had one single dimple on his left cheek and tousled blonde hair. She blinked rapidly and stuffed a fleeting memory quickly back into the recesses of her brain.

"Let's go," Tally said a bit too brusquely. She turned and strode out into the sunlight. The sunlight that managed to chase away the rest of her painful memories.

She led the way over to the cafe with Bobby

12

skipping along beside her and the young woman following closely behind.

They climbed the stairs to the restaurant, and Tereza came hurrying over.

"Tereza, this is Bobby and…" Tally turned to the young woman. "I don't think I caught your name?" Had she just hired a waitress without even knowing her name?

"Courtney. Courtney Davis." The young woman smiled, her blue eyes filled with gratitude.

"Courtney, this is Tereza. Tereza's been here for a few months now. Don't know what I ever did without her. She can show you the ropes."

"But… Bobby."

"Well, we'll work on that, too." Tally motioned to a table. "Sit here. Order what you want." She started to walk away, then looked back. "I'm Tally, by the way. I'll be back in a few minutes."

In all the commotion, she'd managed to forget to grab the box of cloth napkins. She headed to the storage building. She walked inside, crossed through the main room to the storage room, and moved a few boxes around until she found the one she needed. She tugged it off the stack, moved out to the main room, and took a quick look over at the rumpled bed.

She sighed. She knew what she was going to do,

but she didn't want to do it. Not at all. But that wouldn't stop her. She'd still do it. It was the right thing to do.

Courtney was not big at accepting charity, but all she'd had to feed Bobby the last few days was a few leftover peanut butter sandwiches, two apples, and a stale vending machine candy bar. He needed a good, hot meal.

He must have agreed with her decision, because he shoveled the pancakes in with gusto and waved a piece of bacon as he exclaimed how good the breakfast was.

She'd thought she'd turn down the meal for herself but then realized how tired and hungry she was. She couldn't take care of Bobby if she didn't eat, so she'd ordered two eggs and toast. Tereza had also brought them two big glasses of fresh squeezed orange juice and a steaming mug of coffee for Courtney. She sipped the coffee, relishing every delicious sip. Coffee had become a luxury the last few weeks. She'd only spent her money on things for Bobby. Coffee was a want, not a need. Mostly.

She looked over at her son. He'd lost some weight in the last few weeks along with the healthy, tanned cheeks she was used to seeing. Too many days of driving in the car. Hiding out during the day, and driving more at night. They'd snuck into a campground and used the showers there, and one night she'd actually gotten a really cheap hotel room. She'd been exhausted and slept for thirteen hours. Then she'd taken a long, hot bath, chased Bobby into the shower, and they'd gotten back on the road.

Tereza came over to the table. "Can I get you anything else?" Tereza had the faintest hint of a Greek accent and pronounced her name as *Ter-AY-za*.

"No, Tally has been so kind."

Tereza grinned. "Looks like Bobby loves pancakes."

"They're my favorite." Bobby swiped a hand over his sticky mouth.

"So, you said you need someone to watch Bobby while you work? Is he in school yet?"

"Not yet. He just missed the cutoff date. But I do need to find a babysitter."

"Momma, I am *not* a baby."

"Of course you're not. I meant someone to watch you while I work."

Tally walked up to them and set down a big box she was carrying. "Tereza, here are the napkins. I'm not sure how they always seem to disappear, but this should keep us going for a while." Tally turned to Courtney. "So, I'm guessing you need a place to stay?"

Yes, just another of her problems. Childcare, a place to stay, and money. She needed money. "I do, but it can't cost much. I'm, uh, trying to get back on my feet."

"How about free?"

"What?" Courtney stared at the older woman.

"I have that storage building just sitting there. It won't be the first time someone has lived there. It has a small bathroom in the back with a shower. A friend of mine, Julie, used to live there for a while. She fixed it up kind of nice while she was there. It's yours if you want it. There's a small fridge—oh, and there's a microwave. You can use Magic Cafe's kitchen to cook in if you'd like, or you can eat here whenever you want."

"I… I don't know what to say." Hot tears threatened to flood Courtney's eyes. She'd been so stressed, so afraid, so alone for so long. Here was a perfect stranger helping her out.

"Also, we need to go see Dorothy at Belle Island Inn. She has a niece, Belinda, who watches some kids. Let's see if we can work something out for childcare for Bobby." Tally continued solving Courtney's problems.

Courtney jumped up and hugged her, still fighting back tears. Tally awkwardly patted Courtney's back, then stepped away.

Tally cleared her throat. "Now about that car you said was broken down."

"It's out by the bridge to the island."

"Your things are in it?"

"We only got two suitcases, and I have my backpack," Bobby said matter-of-factly.

Courtney hoped that didn't sound too strange to Tally, but that had been all she'd been able to grab when they'd left.

"Well, let's go get your things and get you all settled. Then Tereza can show your mom around Magic Cafe. You think you could keep yourself busy in my office while she does that?"

"I have my books. I can read. And do puzzles."

"He's quite a good reader for his age. And he loves puzzles, especially search-a-word and find the hidden picture."

"All right then. Let's go get your things. I'll have your car towed to the garage. We'll see what Ned says about it."

"But…"

Tally held up a hand. "I know, cash is tight.

We'll just have him look at it to see what he can figure out."

Courtney took Bobby's hand and they followed Tally out of Magic Cafe. She wasn't sure how she'd gotten from absolute desperation when she'd broken into the storage building last night to feeling like her life was somehow going to be a bit easier.

But she was happy for the brief twist of fate no matter how long it lasted.

Susan looked up from the reception area at Belle Island Inn. She was thankful Tally had come to the rescue with Julie's wedding and thankful that she hadn't managed to ruin the day for Julie. Reed would never have forgiven any of them if they'd let Julie postpone the day, either. It had taken long enough for her to pick a date.

She pushed back a lock of hair, then looked at her fingernails. She wasn't sure how she was ever going to get them clean. After scrubbing up so much of the mess from the fire, they seemed permanently etched with soot.

Jamie walked into the lobby. "Hey, Mom. You doing okay today?"

"I'm fine, really. Tally got me all checked out at the clinic yesterday."

Jamie looked like he wasn't quite sure he believed her. "I think you should take it easy today."

"I can't. There is so much to do."

"And I'll help with it."

Susan looked at her son. How had she gotten so lucky to own the inn with him and work with him every day? Life sure had a way of throwing surprises your way when you least expected it. Like when Adam had come to the island just a few short months ago, and now she was married to him. He and his mother, Mary, lived in the cottage beside the inn with her. Even the fire couldn't dampen her feeling of rightness in her world. She felt a smile break across her face.

"What are you smiling about?" Jamie raised an eyebrow.

"I was just thinking how lucky we are."

He nodded. "I hear you on that. We are a very lucky family."

The door opened, and Tally walked into the lobby. A young woman and small boy followed her in. Susan wasn't surprised to see Tally. Her friend was probably checking up on her.

"How are you feeling today?" Tally crossed over

to the reception desk, and Susan came out from behind the desk to greet her.

"I'm doing fine. Really. Everyone should just stop fussing over me."

Jamie snorted. "Right, I'll quit fussing over you when you quit worrying about me."

Susan turned to the young woman standing beside Tally. "I'm sorry. May I help you? Did you need a room?" Thank goodness they'd only had to close two rooms for repair.

"This is Courtney." Tally stepped aside. "And this is Bobby."

The young boy reached out a hand. "Nice to meet you, ma'am."

Susan took his hand, amused at the serious, polite expression on his face. "Nice to meet you, too."

"But Courtney doesn't need a room. She's going to be staying at the storage building behind Magic Cafe."

"Oh, just like Julie used to."

"Just like." Tally nodded. "But we're looking for Dorothy. Bobby is going to need someone to watch him while Courtney works at Magic Cafe."

Susan raised an eyebrow. She'd just seen Tally yesterday. How had all of this happened so quickly? "Dorothy is over at the cottage with Mary. They're knitting." Dorothy had worked the front desk at the inn for years and recently befriended Susan's new mother-in-law. They were both avid knitters and had struck up quite the friendship.

"If you're sure you're okay, I'm going to take Courtney and Bobby over to talk to Dorothy. I know her niece does childcare. I want to see if she has room to take care of Bobby."

"Go right on over. I hope you have luck with Dorothy's niece."

Susan watched her friend lead Courtney and Bobby out the back entrance of the inn. She turned around and saw Jamie staring at her.

"I told you I was okay." She nailed him with her best mother glare.

"I told you that you should take it easy today." He nailed her with his best I'm-not-listening look.

Susan sighed. "I'll go to my office, take it easy, look online, and price out a new grill."

"Good. I've got the front desk until Dorothy comes on duty."

CHAPTER 3

The next afternoon Tally paced along the beach in front of Magic Cafe, trying to figure out the best place to set up a wedding area. Right in front of the restaurant seating area would work, but they'd need to groom the beach a bit and rake up old seaweed. She walked over to the front of the storage building beside the cafe. The beach was level here, and a grove of trees would provide shade while the guests were waiting to be seated. Yes, this area was the best option. Decision made.

She glanced back at the storage building and tilted her head. If Courtney didn't mind, they could use the back room for a place for Julie to get ready. Not fancy, but it did have a big window on the side

23

with lots of natural light. She'd find a full-length mirror for her to use while she was getting ready. Julie could walk right out to the aisle then.

Perfect, that should work. Another decision made. She'd talk to Courtney about it when she got back to the cafe.

Tally walked down to the shoreline and stuck her feet into the water. It was such a calm day that the ocean looked more like a lake than the sea. A peaceful lake. As always, she wondered what her life would be like now if she hadn't been born, raised, and remained on the island. If her family had been from anywhere else, far away from the sea. Or how different it would have been if she'd ever left the island.

But what-ifs never did help things. Her life was what it was. She glanced back to the area of beach by the storage building. Yes, that would work out for Julie.

She was so pleased for her friend. Julie had finally found the happiness she deserved and was finally getting the family she'd always wanted.

If Tally were being really honest, it was hard to see her friends get married and have ever-growing families. She'd never have that. She was finished with family life. Besides, she had good friends, *great* friends. They were all she needed.

She turned back to stare at the tranquil sea. Memories threatened to flood her mind, but she'd long ago learned to keep them at bay, afraid if she ever let them loose, she'd—

"Tally."

That voice. She'd know that voice anywhere. Had her memories burst forth in spite of her best efforts to hide from them?

She slowly turned around and her hand drifted to her mouth. "Eddie."

How many years had it been? Forty or more? He was older now, of course. His hair was sprinkled with gray and a weathered tan covered his face. He was still drop-dead, take-her-breath-away handsome though.

All these thoughts raced through her mind… the mind she seemed incapable of controlling.

Eddie took a step toward her. "I asked in town. They told me you owned Magic Cafe, and I'd probably find you there. A waitress inside told me you were out here."

Eddie looked about as shocked as she felt. His steel blue eyes were narrowed against the bright sun, but he didn't take his gaze off of her.

"What are you doing here?" She didn't know whether to rush forward and hug him or run away and escape. Escape the memories. Escape the rush of feelings soaring through her. She'd never thought she'd see him again. Ever.

"I came looking for you." His familiar voice rolled over her.

"You did? Why? Why now, after all this time?"

"I came looking for my son." Eddie's eyes flashed with determination.

Her heart pounded, and she clenched her fists. His son, the one thing Eddie was searching for, was the one thing Tally couldn't give him.

Edward Williams stood staring at Tally. Oh, how she'd changed. But in a good way. She'd aged into a lovely woman. Her soft gray curls danced in the slight afternoon breeze that had just begun to pick up. She was slender, tanned, and a rosy blush adorned her cheeks. It was all he could do to keep himself from gathering her in his arms.

Well, except for the fact he was mad at her. Very mad. Furious.

"Eddie…"

"No one has called me Eddie in a very long time. I left that person behind when I left Belle Island. I go by Edward now." At least that's what people called him. He still thought of himself as Eddie, but that was kind of ridiculous for a fully grown man of his age.

Tally's eyes were clouded with a dazed expression and she still hadn't taken a step. For a moment he worried she was going to faint, but Tally wasn't the fainting type of person. Though he probably had given her the surprise of her life, showing up here.

His pulse throbbed in his temples. But probably not as big a surprise as he'd been given exactly one week ago when he'd run into an old friend. "I ran into Charlie Moore, remember him?"

Tally's forehead wrinkled, then she nodded.

"Charlie said he'd stayed on the island another few years or so after I left. He mentioned the strangest thing to me." Eddie stood straight and pinned his eyes on Tally. "Charlie mentioned in passing that you'd had a son. He even remembered when he was born. January first, the year after I left. He remembered because there'd been a photo in the paper of the first baby of the year. Your baby."

The color drained from Tally's face.

Eddie pushed on. "I did some quick math, and it didn't take me long to figure out the boy had to be mine. He is, isn't he?"

Tally took a step forward, then covered her face in her hands. "Eddie… I…"

"Charlie couldn't remember his name, though." Eddie's heart thundered in his chest. "What is my son's name?"

"Jackson Edward." Her voice was so low he almost couldn't hear her.

"Jackson *Edward*. I want to meet him. Does he know about me? Know I'm his father?" A red-hot anger flooded through Eddie at all he'd missed, all that had been taken from him. Why hadn't she told him about their son?

Eddie stepped forward and pulled Tally's hands from her face. He tilted her chin up so she had to look right into his eyes. "Why, Tally? Why? And Tally? I want to meet him."

He watched while she swallowed, then licked her lips. "You can't meet him."

"Yes, yes I can."

"No, you can't." A lone tear slid down her cheek and she swiped it away. "You can't because… he's not here anymore."

"Where is he?"

"He's gone… he… died." With that, tears rushed down her face, and she didn't even try to hide them. Raw pain etched her face.

Pain that was mirrored in his own, he was sure.

His knees buckled, and he dropped to kneel in the sand, fighting the searing agony that tore through him.

He'd only just found out that he had a son.

And that son was dead.

CHAPTER 4

Tally knelt on the sand beside Eddie, wanting to reach out and touch him, comfort him, connect with him. But her own agony was too much to bear. She couldn't take on his pain, too.

"I did try to find you, Eddie. I found out I was pregnant after you left town." Tears blinded her eyes as she choked out her words. "I couldn't find you anywhere. When you moved to Dallas, I kept clinging to the hope that you'd write or call. I looked for you, I did. I just had no idea how to find you."

"You could have come with me. I asked you to," he growled at her.

"I know… but I couldn't. I just couldn't." She'd

been unable to take that risk back then—one of the greatest regrets of her life. Her heart squeezed in her chest.

"So you said at the time. I remember the words exactly. 'Not going to happen, Eddie, I'm staying on Belle Island.'" His eyes flashed.

She swiped at the tears rolling down her face. "But I did try to find you after I realized I was pregnant. It's not like it is now with the internet and Facebook and all those ways people keep in contact. I searched for Eddie Smith for years. Do you know how many Eddie, Edward, Ed Smiths there are?"

"I legally changed my name after we moved. To Edward Williams. I took my stepfather's last name. He'd been so good to me for all those years after my father ran out on Mom and me. I also moved on to San Antonio after only a month or so in Dallas. Mom and my stepfather settled down there."

"I guess I was looking for the wrong name, in the wrong town."

"I'm glad you at least were trying to find me." He raked his hands through his hair.

"I wanted you to know you had a son. I did. But then after Jackson…" She paused and steadied her voice. "After he died… well, it seemed pointless to continue to look for you. Why bring that pain to someone else?"

Tally could see the grief etched clearly on Eddie's face.

"How… how did he die? When?"

Tally swallowed. The words tangled in her brain. The pain swelled up inside, threatening to choke her. "He… died at sea. It's been twenty-three years. He was only eighteen. I…" She stopped to catch her breath and fight back the sobs that still threatened to unleash after all this time. "It was right after his first year at college. He was home for summer break. He was so happy, happier than I'd ever seen him. I guess college life agreed with him. The very first morning he was home, he and my father took the boat out fishing. A storm came up quickly. All they ever found were some remains of the boat."

*And no wishes made at Lighthouse Point had brought them back, either.*

Eddie reached out and took her hand. "I'm… so… sorry."

His words wrapped around her like a familiar favorite song. The same voice. The voice that was so similar to Jackson's after he'd grown up and his voice had matured. She stared down at her hand in

33

his, fighting to regain control. The warmth of his hand spread through her, but all she could do was nod at him.

"I know it's hard for you to talk about this, about him. I can see the pain on your face. But, Tally? I want to know more about him. Everything about him." His eyes pleaded with her. "Can I see photos of him? Will you tell me all about him? Can you do that for me?"

Tally looked into his eyes. She would do this for him. He deserved that much. As painful as it would be, she'd tell him everything.

Eddie stood and pulled Tally to her feet. "I need a bit of time to process all this. I'm sure you do, too." He kept her hands in his.

"It has been a bit of a shock to see you after all this time." She looked down at the sand.

The look on her face tore at his heart. Such sadness and pain. "If it's okay with you, I think I'll find a room on the island and stay for a bit. As much as I want to hear everything about my son, I think I need some time first." Time to realize that he'd been so close to having a son, a family, and yet it was all snatched away from him by a trick of the fates.

Tally sucked in a deep breath and squared her shoulders. "You could get a room at Belle Island Inn. My friend, Susan, owns it now."

"I remember the inn."

"It used to be run by her brother. Susan runs it now with her son, Jamie."

"I'll do that, then. I'll get a room for a bit. That will give us both some time."

"That would be... helpful. I do need a bit of time before I can sit and talk about it all. I've done my best for years to just hide from it all. I lost both Jackson and my father. In one horrible day, all my family was gone." Tally slipped her hands from his, and one hand drifted to her heart.

A surge of guilt flooded through him. He should have been here for her. Been there to help raise their son and to help her through the loss of him. But he'd been determined to make a clean break with her when he left Belle Island. He'd had nothing to give her, no future. She'd been a Belle, a member of the founding family of the island. He'd been nobody, with little chance of providing for her. He was sure that's why she'd refused to go with him. She'd been better off without him. At least that's what he'd told himself for years.

Now it looked like his stubborn pride had cost him any chance he'd had for knowing his son. Pain stabbed him, mocked him, pounded him. A wretchedness poured through him, and a pain so raw sucked all the air from his lungs. He bowed his head, then found the strength to look at Tally again.

"I'm so sorry. I should have been here."

"But you didn't know."

"That doesn't make it right."

"Sometimes life just decides to hand you what you don't expect." She scrubbed her hands over her face, then looked up at him. "Come on, let's go get you settled at the inn."

That sounded like a good plan. He needed time to himself. Time to process all that he'd learned today.

Time to let his heart crumble into a million tiny pieces and not let anyone see him fall apart.

Tally watched as Eddie climbed the main stairway at the inn and up to the oceanfront room he'd taken for a week. A *week*. She couldn't quite wrap her head around the fact that he was back in town.

Or the fact that she was going to have to dredge up some very painful memories.

"Are you okay?" Susan walked into the lobby and took a look at Tally, then glanced at Eddie, watching him slowly climb the stairs. "Who is he?" Her friend nodded toward Eddie. "That man you brought to the inn?"

"That's Eddie Smith—I mean, Edward Williams."

"So I take it you know him?"

"I do… well, I did."

"You look really pale. Come sit in my office. Talk to me."

Tally turned to her, struggling to gain control of her emotions. "I… I don't think I can talk about it now."

"Well, now you have me worried." Susan frowned.

"I don't mean to worry you. I don't. I'm sorry. But I need…" Tally looked at the now empty stairway. "I need some time by myself."

"Okay, take the time you need. But I'm always here, day or night. You just call when you want to talk."

Tally continued to stare at the empty stairway. "I will. Maybe we could meet tomorrow at The Sweet Shoppe? Could you call Julie? I'll explain everything then."

"I'll set it up."

Tally nodded. She slowly turned and crossed to the door, escaping out into the fresh air and sunlight. Escaping from the memories and from Eddie and… from Jackson.

CHAPTER 5

Courtney struggled with a heavy tray of food that she needed to deliver to table four. Or was it table five? She needed to look at her order pad to see which table needed the tray, but no way she could reach in the server apron and retrieve the pad with her hands full.

Tereza breezed up and took the tray from her. "You look like you can use some help."

"Thank you." Courtney swiped the pad from the pocket and looked at the order. Table five.

"Don't worry, it gets easier."

"I really have waited tables before… it's just been a really long time. Everything here is different and…"

"It's okay. It will all come back. Before long

you'll know how everything works around here. We don't usually give a new waitress this many tables, but we're short two waitresses tonight. One of them will probably get let go, because this is the second time she's called in at the last minute to cancel this week, and Tally doesn't take kindly to that. She expects workers to be here and expects the best of service for her customers." Tereza balanced the tray. "Okay, what table?"

"Five," Courtney said gratefully.

They crossed over to the table and Tereza bantered with the customers as they served each person. Tereza had a way about her. Friendly and kind, immediately putting the customers at ease, making each one feel like they were her most important customer at Magic Cafe. Courtney could see why Tally had such high praise for her.

At this point, Courtney would be satisfied if she could just get all the orders correct and delivered to the right tables. She and Tereza headed back toward the kitchen.

"You're doing fine." Tereza smiled encouragingly.

"Thanks for the help." Courtney reached for another tray of food, checking to make sure it was one of hers. This one had to be for table four.

"Just shout if you need me." Tereza pushed out

of the kitchen and headed to a group that had just been seated at a large table.

Tereza was doing twice as many tables as she was and handling them with ease. Courtney refused to think about how tired she was and how her feet were killing her. She really needed better shoes to wear if she was going to be a server, but it wasn't in the budget now. So her feet could just keep quiet. She glared at them as if to silence their complaints, then picked up the tray. Table four, the one in the far corner. *Right?*

With a sigh, she pushed out of the kitchen. Hadn't she just been grateful when everything felt like it was falling into place for her? She wondered how Bobby was doing at Belinda's house. She didn't like him out of her sight, but she needed to work, such a catch twenty-two.

Surely all of this would get easier as the days went on like Tereza had said.

Tally thought she wanted to be alone, but that had lasted all of about ten minutes. Instead, she'd gone to Magic Cafe and lost herself in work that night, which was a good thing because they were short staffed. So, she played hostess, server, busboy, and

KAY CORRELL

anything else she could do to keep her brain busy with mindless thoughts. Toward the end of the rush, Paul Clark came into the cafe. He was alone tonight, which didn't happen often. She walked over to his table.

"Hey, Paul. Where's Josephine?"

"My lovely wife went up to Comfort Crossing to visit her sister. I couldn't get away because I have a big gallery showing coming up. It's our first time apart since we got married, and let's just say, it doesn't really agree with me."

"You waited a long time to find her again. I can see how being apart would be difficult."

"It is. She'll be back in two more days, not that I'm counting." He paused and looked at her closely. "Are you okay?"

He knew her so well. They'd been friends for years, ever since he'd come to the island. They'd supported each other through his opening of the gallery and her expanding Magic Cafe. She'd been there when he'd found his long-lost love, Josephine, after fifty-some-odd years. Paul was the one living person who knew about Jackson *and* knew about Eddie. She'd never even told Susan and Julie about them. Jackson had died before either of them had come to town. Oh, they knew she'd had a son that she'd lost, but by tacit agreement, they never talked about it.

But Paul, he'd been there for her back then.

Tally sank into a chair across from him. "It's been a long day."

"And?" he prodded.

She sighed. "Eddie is back. Here on Belle Island."

"Really?" Paul raised an eyebrow. "I thought you couldn't ever find him."

"I couldn't. But he found me."

"So… does he know…" He watched her closely.

"He does. *Now.*" She leaned an elbow on the table and rested her chin on her hand. "He actually came to town because he found out I had a son. He figured out that Jackson was his." She sat back up. "But he hadn't heard that Jackson was… gone."

"Oh, Tally. I'm so sorry. That must have been so hard."

"I feel like I gave him a son, a precious gift, then snatched it away."

"You did try to find him. It's not like it's your fault you couldn't."

"Well, he did move from Dallas where he said he was going, and he changed his last name to his stepfather's last name. Wrong name, wrong city."

"Are you doing okay?"

Tally looked down at her hands. "I'm not really sure. Most of the time I can just keep all the memories tucked away, keeping the pain at bay, but Eddie wants to know everything about Jackson. I can't deny him that. I can't. He deserves that much. Life hasn't been fair to him, either."

"So, you're going to talk to him about Jackson? Are you okay with that? We never talk about him anymore."

"It's just too painful."

"But you're going to talk to Eddie?"

"I am. And I'm going to drag out all those photo albums that I've tucked away. I'm just not sure I'm ready for this…"

"But you'll do it because he's Jackson's father." Paul's eyes were filled with sympathy.

But Tally didn't want sympathy. She wanted… what did she want? Strength to get through this week, day by day?

Survival day by day. It had been so long since she'd lived her life like that. The memories tore at her. Those days after Jackson and her father went missing. Mindlessly watching the hours tick by. Then the days after they'd found the wreckage. She honestly didn't know how she'd made it through those days or how she'd gotten to the place she was now.

But now it looked like all those memories, all the past and the pain were going to be gouged out of the depths of her brain.

So, she'd do like she'd done all those years ago. One day at a time. Until Eddie left. Then she'd be able to go back to her *normal* life.

As if her life would ever be normal.

Tally looked at her friend. "Yes, I will talk to Eddie. Show him the photos. He is Jackson's father, and it's the right thing to do."

Courtney sat on the edge of the twin bed and tugged off Bobby's t-shirt. "Did you have a good time at Belinda's today?"

"I did after the kids got out of school. There's a Mikey, and Stevie, and Billy."

Courtney wondered if when all these boys finally grew up they'd become Mike, Steve, and Bill. Would Bobby become Bob? Or Rob? Or Robert? She snatched her thoughts back to listen to her son tell about his day.

"And we had dinner. Well, just me and Stevie. Mikey and Billy went home before dinner. We had hamburgers and we had to take two bites of the green beans."

Courtney slipped the pajama top onto Bobby's outstretched arms.

Bobby's head popped out of the top of the pj's. "How come they are all in school and I'm not?"

She helped him climb into the pajama bottoms. "You weren't old enough for kindergarten this year. You missed the deadline by a month. You'll go next year."

"How am I going to learn all the stuff I need to know if I'm not in school? Am I gonna go back to pre-kindergarten like I did back home?"

"We'll see about it, Bobby." She doubted she could afford pre-kindergarten and then childcare. Belinda had been very reasonable in her prices. One step at a time. It was probably the wrong time of the year to get him in a pre-k program anyway. She'd need to make time to teach him herself. He was such a sharp kid.

Bobby screwed up his face. "So, is Belle Island home now?"

Courtney sat up straight. How to answer that? She wasn't sure when they'd ever be able to stay in one place for very long. "Well, it is for now, Bobby." She changed the subject. "Go in and brush your teeth, and I'll get you all tucked in."

He trotted off to the bathroom, and Courtney took off her shoes and wiggled her toes. Susan had found an extra rollaway bed at the inn and her son had dropped it off for Bobby. Everyone was so kind to her here. She chastised herself. No point in getting used to it because who knew when she might have to pick up and disappear again. She made up the rollaway with sheets that Susan had also given her.

Bobby came out of the bathroom. "All ready, Momma."

She pulled back the covers, and he climbed into bed. "I like this place. Do you think we can stay for a while? I'm tired of moving around. The car is boring."

"We'll see." She leaned over, kissed him good night, and crossed over to her bed. She sat down and reached for the small velvet pouch on the table beside her bed. She opened the pouch and pulled out a woman's antique rose gold pocket watch she'd found in her mother's things. The watch hung on a thick, gold chain. She didn't know whose it was, but she always felt that it must have been special to her mother. Her mom had kept it in this same velvet pouch. All she had was this and an old folded note that had words and letters, but she couldn't understand what it said. She kept the note anyway.

She slipped the watch around her neck and wrapped her hands around it as it rested against her heart. She'd just sit for a moment before she got ready for bed…

Eddie sat on the balcony of his room at the inn. A light, salty breeze blew in from the water. The moon tossed rays of silver light across the inky shadows of the ocean. He looked far out into the sea, as far as the darkness would allow, searching.

The sea. Something he had always enjoyed, but would never look at in quite the same way. That unending body of water had taken his son, forever sealing his fate. He would never know Jackson. Never hear his voice. Never see him smile.

An unbearable agony tore through him, and he closed his eyes against the pain and the view. A lone tear seared its way down his cheek. He didn't bother to swipe it away. He didn't even have the energy to raise his hand.

The soft sea breeze eventually dried the tear, and he forced himself to open his eyes and look out at the water once again.

Today had not turned out how he had expected. He came here expecting to find his son, to make

Tally pay for keeping his son away from him. Instead, he'd found unbearable pain. Both his and Tally's.

He sat silently and willed himself to get up and go to bed.

But still, he sat in the lonely darkness and looked out at the endless sea—as endless as the pain that now encompassed his very soul.

CHAPTER 6

J ulie finished up the last batch of scones, then peeked out into the dining area of The Sweet Shoppe to see if her friends were here yet. She'd heard the worried tone in Susan's voice when she'd called last night and said they all needed to meet this morning. Something was up with Tally.

It was rare for Tally to be upset by anything. She was always a steady influence in all their lives. Something must be terribly wrong to unsettle her.

Susan walked in and lifted a hand in a brief wave. Julie motioned to the table in the corner and Susan nodded.

Julie pulled the last sheet of scones from the oven and set them on a rack to cool. She snatched off her apron, dished up three piping hot scones, and pushed through the swinging door to join her friend.

"Raspberry," Julie said as she set the scones on the table. "Be right back with coffee." She hurried back with three mugs of coffee and sat down across from Susan. "So, Tally was really upset?"

"She was, and that's not like her. I can't imagine what in the world could unsettle her like that. She was actually pale. I couldn't get her to talk."

"You think something is wrong with her health? The Magic Cafe is doing well, I doubt if it's something to do with that." Julie frowned and took a sip of her coffee. "Maybe she's having second thoughts about having the wedding at Magic Cafe."

"Maybe?" Susan looked skeptical.

The door opened, and Tally stepped inside, pausing to look around the room. She nodded when she saw them waiting for her.

She slipped into a chair at the table. "Morning."

"I baked raspberry scones." Julie pointed to the treats. "I snagged us three before they get sold out to my customers. These and the almond scones always seem to go first."

"Thanks." Tally reached for one and took a bite. She looked at Julie and Susan and sighed. "Okay, it's kind of a long story."

"We have time." Susan leaned forward.

"You know I lost my son years ago." Tally's eyes betrayed the pain she tried to hide.

"We do. But you never talk about him, so…" Julie trailed off.

"He was lost at sea with your father, right?" Susan's voice was almost a whisper.

"Yes, they both died during a storm a sea. Jackson, my son, was eighteen at the time."

Susan reached over and touched Tally's strong, weathered hand. "It must have been so hard to lose a son. I can't imagine. And to lose your father at the same time."

"They were all the family I had left." Tally stared down at Susan's hand on hers. "It was… so hard. Nearly impossible. I just tried to make it through each day, hour by hour. At first, everyone who saw me would say how sorry they were for my loss. I got so I could barely tolerate leaving our cottage. I couldn't bear to hear those words. Eventually, I threw myself into running Magic Cafe. Kept myself busy every minute, long into the night. The nights were the worst."

The few wrinkles around Tally's eyes deepened as she struggled to stay composed.

"I got so I didn't speak about it to anyone, and eventually people quit talking about it. I put it behind me and moved on. Life sometimes throws you a tough one, but you do eventually have to move on and live your life." Tally pulled her hand from Susan's and rubbed it across her face. "I haven't even talked to you two about it, and you're my best friends. It happened before either of you came, so… it was just easier not to say anything."

"But yesterday you were so upset." Susan's forehead wrinkled. "What happened?"

"Well, that's the other part of the story. Jackson's father." Tally sighed. "The town thinks Jackson's father is some man who died in an accident before my son was born. It… well, it was sort of a rumor my father started to protect Jackson. Most people thought I went away and got married and lost my husband. I left town after I got pregnant and went to live with my aunt, but she got sick and I came back to Belle Island to have my baby. When I got back here, the rumor was already spread, and no one mentioned it. Maybe people believed it, maybe not, but they sure wouldn't say anything to me. My father helped me raise Jackson. He was wonderful with him."

"So who is Jackson's father?" Julie took a swallow of coffee.

"His name is Eddie Smith. Well, he goes by Edward Williams now. He came to town yesterday looking for me." Tally let out a long breath. "He ran into an old friend from the island and found out I had a son. You see, Jackson was the first baby born that year and had his photo in the paper and, well, Eddie did the math and figured out Jackson was his."

"You never told him you were pregnant?" Susan raised an eyebrow.

"He left town before I found out. Then, I couldn't find him. I tried. My father tried. But we didn't have any luck." Tally's face clouded. "Eddie's friend had left town years ago and didn't know that Jackson had died. So Eddie came here hoping…"She rubbed her face again. "He was hoping to meet his son."

"Oh, Tally. That's horrible. He must have been devastated." Susan's eyes widened.

"He was. He is."

Julie frowned. She'd known Tally for so many years, and yet, here was a total surprise about her. Julie wasn't sure how she felt about that. Why hadn't Tally spoken about Eddie before this? "So, he's staying here for a while?"

"He is. He wants me to…" She shook her head. "He wants me to tell him all about Jackson. What he was like. Show him photos."

"Are you okay with that?" Julie looked at her

friend. Her friend she'd known for so many years had never said one word about her son.

"Well, Eddie deserves that much. None of this is his fault. It's just some quirk of the universe that brought us to this point."

Susan leaned forward again and took Tally's hand. "I think maybe, just maybe, it might be good for you to talk about Jackson. Share his life with Eddie. Maybe it will help you deal with your pain if you have someone to share it with."

Tally watched as Courtney and Bobby played out on the beach later that morning. Bobby raced the waves and Courtney laughed at his antics. Tally smiled in spite of herself. Bobby had so much energy, always dashing around, but he was remarkably polite and well behaved.

He reminded her so much of Jackson.

That thought froze her in place. Thoughts like that just didn't pop into her head. They were kept tucked neatly away, far from consciousness. Eddie had stirred things up, and she wasn't sure she was ready to have Jackson pop into her mind unexpectedly and often.

Courtney took Bobby's hand, and they walked

up toward Magic Cafe. Bobby waved at Tally and dashed ahead of his mother and up to where Tally was standing.

"Miss Tally, did you see me racing the waves? I won." He puffed out his chest.

"I did see that."

Courtney reached them. "Bobby loves the beach. This is the first time he's ever been to the ocean."

"It's super fun and I don't ever wanna leave." He nodded his head eagerly. "It's like the best place ever, right, Momma? I want this to be our home now."

A look flashed across Courtney's face, but Tally couldn't quite tell what it was. Disappointment? Confusion? The woman quickly hid it and smiled.

Bobby's enthusiasm was infectious, and Tally couldn't help but smile, too. Oh, to see every day as a grand adventure.

"It is pretty nice here." Courtney watched her son as he danced from foot to foot.

"And there's lots of nice people. Like Miss Belinda and Stevie." Bobby stopped hopping around. "Oh, and you, too, Miss Tally. Momma and I like our new apartment."

Tally wouldn't exactly call the storage building an apartment, but it did seem to serve its purpose of providing Courtney and her son a free place to stay.

"I really do appreciate all the help you've given us." Courtney's eyes were filled with gratitude.

"Glad I could help." Everyone deserved a bit of help when life was tough. Tally knew that better than most. She'd thought it would be difficult to have a young boy around, but Bobby was hard to resist.

The boy grabbed his mother's hand and tugged. "Come on. We have to go get ready for Miss Belinda's. You said you gotta work soon and I want to get there and play with the guys."

"I won't be late for my shift," Courtney assured Tally.

"I'll see you then." Tally stood and watched as Bobby ran circles around his mother while they headed over to the storage building. The boy was a whirlwind of motion.

"Who's that?"

Tally twirled around at the sound of Eddie's voice. "I… hi. That's Courtney and her son, Bobby. She's a new waitress I hired."

"The boy looks like a firecracker."

"I'm pretty sure he is."

Silence dropped between them. Tally knew

Eddie was eager to talk, to ask questions, but he remained silent.

She squared her shoulders and drew in a deep breath for courage. "Jackson was just like that at that age. Constant energy. I sometimes can't believe I could ever keep up with him."

Eddie turned to her, encouraging her to talk with the look of gratitude in his eyes.

"Jackson loved living here on Belle Island. He could swim almost before he could walk." Not that it had saved him. She pushed the thought of the horrible death her son had endured aside. "He was smart, too. He could read before he started school and was a whiz at math. He loved to learn. Anything that caught his attention." Tally motioned to chairs at the edge of the beach and they both sat. She kicked off her shoes and dug her feet into the warm sand.

"What do you want to know about him? I just have all these random thoughts and I don't really know what to tell you."

"What did he look like?" Eddie's voice and the edge of pain it held washed over her.

"He... was handsome. I know every mom thinks that, but he was. He had your thick, wavy hair, and he had your eyes. I often could see a lot of you in him.

He was short though, not tall like you. Never hit a good growth spurt. Played a lot of sports and good at them, but not best-on-team good. He worked hard at getting good grades." Tally leaned back in the chair and closed her eyes. "He had a quick smile and a way of biting his lower lip when he was concentrating. He had a scar above his left eye from when he slipped in the tub as a young boy. I've never seen something bleed so badly and I felt like a horrible mother for letting it happen. The scar reminded me all the time of how quickly things can happen…"

Eddie looked over at Tally sitting beside him with her eyes closed. The sun bathed her face, highlighting a few small wrinkles around her eyes. She'd aged, had a hard life, but she… she still reminded him so much of the young girl he'd left behind. "Did everyone call him Jackson? Or did they nickname him, Jack?"

"Everyone called him Jackson. Not sure why it was never shortened. He seemed like a Jackson, though."

"And you gave him my name as his middle name?"

"I did." Tally's voice was low. "I considered

naming him Edward for his first name but changed my mind. The town thought I'd gotten married when I moved away for a while when I was pregnant. I stayed with my aunt. I think my father started a vague rumor about how my husband had been killed in an accident. He thought it would be easier for Jackson that way."

"But you moved back here to have your baby? Charlie said that Jackson was the first baby of the year."

"My aunt got sick and I did move back here. I had Jackson on Belle Island. We both lived with my father. He seemed to enjoy having us there, and it was easier for me to work, knowing that my father was there to help with Jackson." She opened her eyes and turned to look at him. "Dad was great with Jackson. They were best of friends."

"And you lost both of them at the same time." Eddie couldn't imagine the pain Tally had gone through.

She nodded and looked away. "It was… hard. Incredibly hard."

He didn't say anything, giving her time to collect her thoughts.

"But life isn't always fair, is it?" She looked back at him. "You never even got to meet him."

A pain gripped Edward's heart. The pain of loss.

The pain of what-ifs. "I wish…" He looked at Tally. "I wish you would have come with me when I asked you. Everything would have been so different."

She looked directly into his eyes, pain painted across every inch of her face. "You think I haven't thought of that? How my one decision changed everything?"

"I'm not blaming you, Tally." He reached out and covered her hand. "I'm not. I know you felt like you couldn't leave your father alone. And I know that Belle Island is as much a part of you as your heart and your very being. I understood." And he'd had nothing to offer her at that point. Nothing.

"But if I'd been willing to take that chance, take that risk…"

"There are a lot of what-ifs in life, but the thing is, they don't really change anything. We make the decisions we make and live with the consequences. I could have stayed here instead of moving to Texas for that job. You know, the one that I thought would be my big break? *Right.* That job that turned out to be a colossal mistake, so I moved down to San Antonio near my mom and stepfather. That's when I changed my name. My stepfather had always been so good to me and my mother. He was really the only dad I ever knew. It seemed like the right thing to do at the time. But it probably sealed it that you'd never find me." Eddie stared out at the waves, at the ocean that had stolen his son. Would he ever be able to look out at the sea without thinking that thought?

"You had no way to know that I was looking for you."

Decisions. Choices. How they could change a person's life forever. "I could have come back to find you. Come back before now. But… I just thought I had nothing to offer you. And my pride. When we're young our pride really gets in our way, doesn't it? I was hurt that you wouldn't come with me, and I thought part of it was because… well, I thought I wasn't good enough for you."

"It was never that, Eddie. Ever." Tally looked out at the horizon. "I just couldn't leave the island. I couldn't even leave after this blasted ocean took everything away from me."

CHAPTER 7

At lunchtime Tally looked up, surprised to see Camille Montgomery standing at the hostess station. Since Camille's family had put their house on the rental market, Tally had thought they might have seen the end of her. Tally put on her best welcoming smile and crossed over to her. She still hadn't totally forgiven the woman for how she'd accused Julie of stealing silver from her house when Julie had catered an event for the Montgomerys. It had all turned out okay, though, when Reed had discovered the real thief. Not that Camille had apologized for all the trouble she'd caused Julie. Not that Camille was one to apologize for anything…

"Camille, just one?"

"No, of course not." She said it like it was the

craziest thing ever to dine alone. "Delbert is meeting me here."

"Okay, a table for two."

"But not too close to the edge of the deck. It's so sandy there."

Tally wondered why Camille would come to a beach cafe if she didn't like the beach, but kept the thought to herself and led Camille to a table near the middle of the dining area. Camille looked around as if trying to figure out if the table met with her standards. She finally nodded and slipped into her chair.

"Miss Tally. Miss Tally." Bobby came running up. "Look what I found but I'm gonna put it back in the ocean so it doesn't die but I wanted to show you." Bobby's sentence ran together in one long string of words, then he held up a starfish. "See?"

He bumped against Camille's table in his exuberance, and the menu and silverware napkin roll spilled to the floor.

"Goodness. Watch what you're doing." Camille scooted her chair back.

Bobby's eyes opened wide. "I'm sorry, lady."

Tally intervened. "It's okay, Bobby. It was an accident."

Courtney came hurrying up. "Bobby, don't disturb Miss Tally and her customers."

"I wanted her to see my starfish."

"When I said you could show her, I didn't mean to interrupt her work."

Tally put her hand on his shoulder. "He's never interrupting me. He's welcome at any time."

"You'll get me a new napkin, right? That one has been on the floor."

"Of course," Tally said patiently to Camille. *Her words did sound patient, didn't they?* Maybe.

"That looks like a mighty fine starfish, son." Delbert Hamilton walked up beside them.

"Thanks. I think so. It's my first ever one I've found." Bobby held out his hand for Mr. Hamilton to see.

"Yep, one of the finest I've seen." Mr. Hamilton carefully touched the starfish. Camille grimaced when he did.

"I'm gonna go put it back in the sea now."

"That's a good idea." Mr. Hamilton nodded gravely.

"'Cause I don't wanna kill it."

"Yep, that would be bad," Mr. Hamilton agreed.

"Come on, Bobby, let's leave everyone to their lunch."

"It was nice meeting you… what's your name, son?" Mr. Hamilton smiled at Bobby.

"Bobby. My name's Bobby."

"Nice meeting you, *Bobby*." Mr. Hamilton reached out to shake his non-starfish hand.

Courtney led Bobby back to the beach, and Tally turned her attention to Camille and Mr. Hamilton.

An appalled look crossed Camille's face when Mr. Hamilton took his seat. "Delbert, are you going to go wash your hand after touching that creature?"

The man threw back his head and laughed. "No, Camille. I'm pretty sure I'm going to live if I eat after touching a starfish."

Camille huffed then turned to Tally. "A new napkin?" She looked pointedly at the one on the ground.

Delbert reached down and swooped up the napkin roll. "This one's fine for me."

"Delbert, sometimes I think you are positively barbaric."

He winked. "Part of my charm, I'm sure."

Tally hurried off to retrieve a new napkin and send Tereza over to get their order. She'd pretty much hit her limit with being patient with Camille for the day. Or the week.

That evening Courtney picked up a large tray of

food and pushed through the door from the kitchen to the restaurant. Table six. She smiled to herself. She'd at least learned to look at the table number in advance of picking up the tray. As she glanced around the deck, she froze. A man in uniform was talking to Tally. Some kind of policeman. Her pulse quickened, and she looked left and right for an escape route.

Courtney whirled around and rushed back into the kitchen, her heart pounding. Tereza looked up from where she was pulling a rack of glasses from the dishwasher. "You okay?"

"I… I'm just not feeling well."

"Let me take that food out for you."

"Thanks. Table six." Courtney handed her the tray.

"Sit down on that chair for a minute. I'll be right back." Tereza disappeared with the food.

Courtney sank onto the chair. She couldn't hide in here all night. Maybe the officer would leave?

Tereza came back to the kitchen. "You look pale."

"No, I'm okay. I think I'm just tired." She stood. She needed this job. She couldn't say she was sick and hide. She wanted Tally to know she was dependable. She needed the wages from every hour she worked and every single tip she could manage.

She walked to the doorway and saw the man was no longer talking to Tally. Relief swelled through her. Time to get back to work.

"You've got table four now. You sure you're okay? I could take it." Tereza's eyes were filled with concern.

"No, I'm fine. Thanks."

Courtney hurried over to table four and took out her order pad. "May I…" She froze. The uniformed man sat at the table. Her table.

He looked up and smiled at her. "You must be new here."

"Y—yes, I am."

"I'm Sheriff Dave. Welcome to Belle Island."

"Thanks. May I take your order?" No way she was offering up her name.

"I'll have crab cakes and a large iced tea. Oh, and a side of hushpuppies."

She scribbled the order, nodded, and whirled away. She fled to the kitchen and leaned against the wall. Now, what was she going to do? She had to act normal. She didn't want to arouse suspicion.

Tereza entered the kitchen and took one look at her. "Okay, what's going on? You look pale again. Are you okay?"

"I… can you take table four for me?"

"Sheriff Dave's table?" Tereza narrowed her eyes. "Are you in some kind of trouble?"

"No... I..." Courtney didn't want to explain. Not even to these people who had been so kind and generous to her. Some things were better kept secret.

Tereza paused then held out her hand. "I'll take his table. Give me his order, I'll put it in."

She handed her the scribbled order.

Tereza turned, then paused and looked back at Courtney. "I'm here if you ever need to talk."

Courtney sank onto the chair and tucked her hair behind her ear. The hair that was much shorter now than before, and no longer the stand-out-in-a-crowd golden blonde she'd been born with. She'd dyed it an unremarkable shade of brown and chopped it a good six inches to shoulder length. Just long enough to pull back. She knew she looked different now.

But did she look different enough?

CHAPTER 8

Tally came out of the storage building where she'd been making sure they had enough champagne glasses for Julie's wedding. Mary, Susan's mother-in-law, came walking up the beach with Stormy, the pup she'd rescued during a storm earlier this year. Mary waved and crossed over to Tally. Stormy wagged his tail as if Tally was the most exciting thing he'd ever seen. She reached down and petted the pup.

"Beautiful day for a walk."

"I've been walking Stormy every day. He has so much energy. My son, Adam, makes me keep him on a leash though. He's afraid Stormy will run off like when I found him in the storm. He also makes me carry my phone with me. There's some kind of tracker app on it." Mary turned in a circle to get the leash untangled from around her legs. "I know he worries about me, but I'm fine."

Tally wondered what it was like to know you had Alzheimer's and that you were starting to forget things but wanting so badly to maintain a normal life for as long as possible. "Sounds like the app on your phone is a way to keep him from worrying so much."

Mary sighed. "I don't want him to worry, but I'm not willing to be… well, I like my walks and don't plan on giving them up anytime soon."

"Miss Tally. Miss Tally." Bobby came running up the beach. He dropped to the sand beside Stormy, and the dog began licking his face. Bobby giggled. "What's his name?"

"Stormy." Mary grinned at the boy and the dog.

"I don't have a dog. Always wanted one but Momma says no."

Courtney trotted up to them. "I swear I can't keep up with this kid. Wish I had his energy."

"Mary, you remember Courtney and Bobby from when we stopped by the inn to talk to Dorothy. They are staying here, and Courtney is working at Magic Cafe."

"I remember." Mary turned around again to unwrap the leash Stormy had wound around her.

"Momma, isn't this the best dog ever?" Bobby fell back on the sand and Stormy climbed on his chest.

"Best one, ever." Courtney grinned at her son.

"Hey, Miss Mary, can I walk Stormy?"

Mary looked at Courtney. "I was just going to walk a short way down the beach. Bobby is welcome to come with us."

Tally saw that same look flash across Courtney's face. The one she couldn't quite figure out.

"I…" Courtney looked at Tally.

"I was thinking of getting in a short beach walk myself. How about we take Bobby with us and we'll bring him back here when we're finished? Mind if I join you, Mary?"

"That would be nice." Mary smiled.

Courtney slowly nodded in agreement. "Bobby, you behave and listen to Miss Tally."

"Yes." He did a quick fist pump. "I'll listen, I promise, Momma."

Mary reached out and handed Bobby the leash. "Slip your hand through the loop to make sure you don't drop it."

"Come on, Stormy. Let's go race the waves." Bobby took off toward the shoreline.

"Bobby, slow down," Courtney called after him. "Wait for Miss Mary and Miss Tally."

He slowed down the tiniest bit.

"We'll keep an eye on him. We'll be back soon, don't worry," Tally assured Courtney to allay her fears. But then, what kind of mother didn't worry about their son?

Courtney watched as Tally and Mary walked away. Bobby and Stormy raced back and forth near the women. Her heart tripped watching him meander away from her, getting tiny in the distance the farther they walked. It was so hard to let him out of her sight. It was hard enough to leave him with Belinda, but she really had no choice.

Courtney turned to go into the storage building, their home for now. It did seem almost like home after only a few days. She wasn't sure how that had happened so quickly.

Bobby was so happy here on Belle Island. So carefree. She hadn't seen him like that in a long time. The haunted look was almost gone from his face, though he still was having nightmares. They hadn't ended.

*She* was still having nightmares. She'd wake up from them and jump up and check that Bobby was okay, looking down at his innocent face. She'd do anything to protect him, anything.

Even kidnap him.

CHAPTER 9

Eddie waited until the lunch crowd died down at Magic Cafe and went to find Tally. He was hoping they could talk again. He was even toying with the idea of taking her to dinner.

She looked up when she saw him, and for a brief moment, she was that young girl again. The one who had that special smile, just for him. The years simply slipped away.

A sad looked crept over Tally's face, and all those years came crashing back with a vengeance. So much had changed. He was still reeling from everything he'd found out this past week.

Jackson. Just thinking his name made his heart ache.

He lifted a hand with a quick wave and climbed the stairs to the outside seating area. "Hey."

"Did you come for lunch?" Tally pushed away a wayward lock of hair.

He had to keep from staring at her hands. They'd aged, too. A bit weathered and wrinkled, but still incredibly strong and capable. Tally was an enigma. Exactly the same and yet so different.

She repeated her question. "Lunch?"

Oh, he hadn't answered her. "No, I came to see…" All of a sudden he was uncertain. As nervous as he'd been the first time he'd asked her out all those years ago. "Um… would you like to go out to dinner tonight?"

Tally's eyes widened. "I… well, I work every night here at Magic Cafe."

"You don't ever take time off?"

"Very, *very* rarely."

"Could this be one of those rare times?" He winked at her.

"I… I don't know. I'd have to check and see who's on the schedule. Make sure everything is covered."

Eddie dropped into a chair, stretched out his legs, and crossed his arms. "I'll wait. Go check."

She stood for a moment, then nodded and headed away.

He told himself he wouldn't be disappointed if she said no. He knew she was busy running Magic Cafe. So, of course, there'd be no disappointment. None.

He stared at the direction she'd headed, wondering how long it would take her to come back and put him out of his misery. A simple yes or no, preferably yes.

She returned after about ten minutes. Ten long minutes.

"Well?" He looked up at her.

"Tereza is working and so is Courtney. Along with a couple other good employees. I could probably get away." Tally's voice didn't sound very confident or excited to be going out with him.

He refused to let her lack of enthusiasm deter him. He jumped up. "Perfect. What time should I pick you up?"

"Well, I was thinking..."

He tilted his head. Was she going to back out?

"I never eat dinner at home. I'm always here at Magic Cafe. I wouldn't mind cooking a simple meal for you if that sounds okay?"

He'd eat anywhere and eat anything. He was just glad she'd said yes. "I don't want you to go to any trouble... but if that's what you want, that sounds great."

"You could come about six?"

"And you live…?"

"I'm still in the same house, the one I grew up in. I never could bring myself to move."

"Got it. I'll be there at six." Eddie turned to leave, hope planted firmly in his chest that they'd have a great evening. He quickened his steps and disappeared down the beach before she could change her mind.

Tally looked around the kitchen at the same fading paint and the same worn table. She'd changed nothing over the years. It had been forever since she'd actually cooked a dinner at home. She usually just grabbed something at Magic Cafe. After Jackson and her father were… gone… she couldn't tolerate sitting alone at the empty table. So she didn't. When she did eat at home, she often ate standing at the sink, looking out the window.

But tonight she was cooking again. She'd made a roasted chicken with rosemary sauce, a simple salad, and fresh green beans. Nothing fancy.

She looked at the clock. Five-forty. She had time to change. She looked down at her worn slacks and sandals. The pants were probably ten years old, or maybe older than that. She rarely shopped for new clothes. What should she wear tonight and why did she even care?

She hurried to her bedroom and slid open the closet door. Worn jeans, a few casual skirts, and a handful of dresses reserved for weddings or special events. She grabbed a simple skirt and blouse and changed into them. A quick brushing of her hair, and she called it good. Well, as good as it was going to get. She looked in the mirror and then tugged open the bathroom drawer. After rooting around, she found some eye makeup and quickly applied some. When was the last time she'd worn makeup? And why was she using makeup tonight? It wasn't a date. Eddie was just coming over to dinner. Right? She resolutely closed the drawer and turned out the light.

Two minutes until six.

She hurried to the kitchen and checked the chicken. The doorbells rang, and she took one last look around the hastily picked up kitchen. She crossed over the worn plank floor and tugged open the door.

Eddie stood in the doorway, his tall frame filling the opening. He'd dressed in slacks and a button-down shirt, with the sleeves rolled up. He held a bouquet of flowers out for her. "Here you go. You used to love flowers."

No one had given her flowers in… how many years? Jackson used to bring her flowers for no reason. He always said they were just because he was so lucky to have her as a mom, though usually they were because he'd gotten into some kind of minor trouble and wanted to butter her up to get her to forgive him. Which she always did, of course. Her heart clenched in her chest. She reached out and took the flowers with shaky hands. "Thank you. Come in."

Eddie followed her into the house. "Still looks about the same."

"I know. I keep thinking I'll get it all painted and replace some furniture, but never seem to make the time."

He followed her into the kitchen. "Smells wonderful."

"It's rosemary chicken." The flowers added a cheerful splash to the room when she arranged them in a vase that she placed on the table. She looked around the kitchen with a critical eye. It did need new paint. Maybe a subtle yellow to brighten it up. The curtains were years old and certainly should be replaced. She was so rarely home that she hadn't put much thought or energy into keeping up with more than just major repairs. She made up her mind to do something about it.

Probably…

She turned to Eddie. "Would you like a beer or some wine?"

"A beer would be good."

She grabbed a beer for Eddie and poured herself a glass of wine. "Let's go sit in the front room."

They settled on the worn couch and Eddie took a swig of his beer. Silence stagnated the surrounding air.

Eddie sat awkwardly on the sofa, glancing around the room, trying to think of something to say. Tally sat perched on the edge of the sofa beside him. For the life of him, he couldn't get the thought out of his mind that she looked ready to run.

"So I—"

"Would you—"

They both spoke at the same time. Eddie laughed. "No, go ahead."

"I wondered if you'd like to see a photo album. Some pictures of Jackson."

"I would." He set his beer on a coaster on the coffee table. "I'd like that a lot."

Tally got up and walked over to the bookcase. She reached up and ran her hand over the covers of a row of albums as if caressing a beloved keepsake. She pulled one off the shelf and came over to sit beside him again.

He watched as she slowly opened the album, allowing access to a whole new world for him. His breath caught in his chest.

"This was Jackson as a baby. About nine months old."

Eddie reached out to touch the photo, to connect to his son. His heart shattered, and he fought for his breath. "Jackson." His voice was a whisper.

Tally looked at him, her face reflecting his own pain. "Do you want to keep going?"

He nodded, unable to speak.

"This was when he lost his first tooth. I love this big grin of his." She turned the page. "Here is one from when my father took him deep sea fishing. The fish is bigger than Jackson."

Tally kept turning the pages, commenting on each photo. Eddie sank into his son's world, cherishing each tiny glimpse of his life while regretting missing each day, each moment.

Tally closed the album. "Is that enough for now? I…"

Eddie looked at Tally and knew she'd had enough for tonight. Her hand rested lovingly on the cover of the album and tears filled the corners of her eyes.

"Thank you for sharing those with me."

"I have more. Lots more. But maybe we could do those another time?" Her voice shook. "It's been a long time since I've gone through these."

"Yes, another time." Eddie leaned forward. "Could I take this back to the inn with me? I'll bring it back. I'd just like to… look at the photos again." And again, and again. Memorize each smile, the one dimple, the toothless grin.

Tally's hands tightened around the album.

"I'll bring it back, I promise."

"We should probably get some of these photos scanned for you." Tally still held the album. "If you'd like that."

"I would."

"Susan has a scanner at the inn. I'm sure she'd let you use it. It can scan to a thumb drive."

"I'll pick up a thumb drive and see if Susan will let me use the scanner." He wanted to scan each and every single photo in the album. As if that could bring him any closer to all he'd missed in his son's world.

∼

Tally leaned against the worn door after Eddie left. They'd had a pleasant, if awkward at times, dinner. She had a hard time letting Eddie leave with the album. Which was ridiculous, because she never took it out and looked at the photos—she hadn't in years. But it was strangely comforting to have them sitting on her bookcase.

She shook her head at her thoughts. She was a silly old woman. Eddie would bring the album back. He'd have his scanned photos. It would be okay.

She glanced over at the open slot on the bookcase where the album had been. She crossed over and picked up a framed photograph of her father and Jackson, one of the few photographs she kept out. Jackson was about six and was looking up at her father with such adoration in his eyes. It was one of her favorite photos of him. She traced the outline of his face with her index finger.

She set the photo back on the shelf and walked over to switch out the light. She stood in the darkness, lost in memories.

She'd planned on taking Eddie up to Jackson's room. The room still looked the same. She hadn't been able to do anything with it. It still had fading posters on the walls and a shelf of trophies. His favorite bat leaned against the wall in the corner. But she just hadn't been able to go up there with Eddie. Not yet. But she would. She knew that Eddie would love to see the room.

Next time. She needed a few days to prepare herself. She'd kept the door firmly shut for years, rarely going in. A few times, though, in spite of her best intentions, she'd gone up to his room in the middle of the night when she couldn't sleep and lay down on his bed, staring at the ceiling, railing at the fates.

Not that it did any good.

Jackson was still gone. Her father was gone. She was the only one left in a long line of the Belle family.

CHAPTER 10

The next day after the breakfast crowd had thinned, Tally sat at a table with Courtney making up napkin rolls for the tables. They grabbed a knife, fork, and spoon and rolled each set in a napkin. She could tell Courtney welcomed the break to get off her feet for a bit. The girl needed to get new shoes, that's for sure, but she doubted Courtney would spend that money on herself.

"So where are you from, Courtney?"

A shadow flitted across her face. "Oh, here and there. We've moved a lot."

"I've lived here my whole life."

"Really? You've never lived anywhere else?" Courtney looked surprised.

"Nope, never." Tally rolled another napkin. "You have any family?"

"No." Courtney looked down and concentrated on meticulously picking out exactly the right knife, fork, and spoon.

Tally knew vague when she heard it. "Just you and Bobby?"

"My grandmother raised me. She died when I was eighteen."

"I'm sorry."

"Don't be. She… well, she wasn't very happy to be raising me and let me know it at every opportunity." Courtney bit her lip, like she was sorry all that had tumbled out. Her face held a stony mask, struggling to pretend it didn't matter.

"That must have been hard."

"Not really. It's all I knew." She reached for a napkin. "I'm trying to be a better mother to Bobby than what I had growing up."

Tally could see that Courtney was a good mother. Lots of hugs for Bobby and laughter. She played with him, and the other day she heard Courtney teaching him to count by fives. A person could tell just by looking at them that Courtney adored her son.

"Anyway, I want him to know that he's wanted.

That I love him." She shrugged. "I think that's what every child wants."

"I think so, too."

Tereza came up to the table. "That order of wine is here."

Tally got up. "I'll go check it. Thanks."

"I'll help Courtney finish these up. My last table just left."

Tally walked away but paused and looked back at the two girls chatting with each other. It would do Courtney good to have a friend here in town, and Tereza was just the person to take on the job.

Courtney rolled another napkin and turned the conversation to the weather. She hoped Tereza wouldn't ask questions about the other night—the night when she'd been hiding out from Sheriff Dave. Just thinking about him made her take a quick look around the cafe. She wasn't sure she would ever feel safe again. She hoped she was making it so Bobby felt safe, though, protecting him as best she could.

She always worried if she was a good mother. It's not like she'd had a good role model. Her grandmother had always let her know that it was her fault her mother was gone. Her mother had died in childbirth and Courtney had survived. As far as her grandmother was concerned, Courtney had killed her own mother. As she got older, she realized it wasn't really her fault, but it did always nag in the back of her mind that if not for her, her mother would still be alive.

"You okay?" Tereza added a napkin roll to the pile. "You look lost in thought."

"Oh, just thinking."

"About what?"

"Mostly about Bobby."

"He's a great kid." Tereza grinned. "He's got a lot of energy though. I get tired just watching him zip around."

"He never does stop. Until he does. He drops off quickly at night and sleeps like a rock. He is a great kid though. I'm a lucky mom."

"Does he like going to Belinda's?"

"He does, especially when the other boys are there in the afternoon after school. He can't wait to start school." Though she had no idea where they'd be this fall when school started back up. She kept reminding herself that they couldn't stay here for long. She'd just save up as much as she could, then they'd move on.

"You have that look on your face again." Tereza frowned

"What look?"

"The one that says you're worried about something."

"Ah… no, I'm not worried about anything. Well, a bit about money, but this job is helping with that."

"You sure that's all it is? Not that money problems aren't a big deal."

"That's all." Along with hiding out and making sure she and Bobby couldn't be found. But she wasn't going to share that worry with Tereza no matter how kind her new friend was to her.

CHAPTER 11

Julie sat out on the deck of their beach house with Reed. She really should be doing something wedding-wise, but exhaustion crept into her very bones. Besides just normal working at The Sweet Shoppe today, she'd baked two large cakes for events in town—an anniversary party and a sweet sixteen party. But the wedding was one week away. She should be doing *something* for it because the to-do list was certainly long enough.

"You look tired." Reed squeezed her hand. "You work too hard."

"No such thing as working too hard." She held up a hand. "And don't offer to help out with The Sweet Shoppe. I have to do it on my own."

"I know. The offer is always there though. I can get you new ovens, hire more help."

"Reed, some things aren't about money." Julie shot the words back at him, then instantly regretted it. She reached out to touch his hand. "I'm sorry. I'm tired and stressed. I appreciate your offer of help, but I really need The Sweet Shoppe to be my own thing. Make it successful on my own."

"It is successful."

"I want to make sure it stays that way." She sipped her wine. "I don't mean to be short with you. I don't know what's come over me this last month."

"What's stressing you? I want to help you in any way you'll let me."

Reed was always so patient, always so understanding. How could she tell him the wedding was stressing her out? Of course, weddings were supposed to be stressful, weren't they?

"Julie?"

She sighed. "I admit I'm nervous about meeting all your friends and co-workers who are coming. You're from such a different world than me. Your friends are probably going to wonder what you ever saw in me. And it's not going to be a real fancy wedding, the kind you're used to going to. And I really don't like to be the center of attention." Julie blurted it all out at once but then wanted to take the words back.

"I would be perfectly content to run off with you and get married." Reed leaned over and kissed her. "I don't need a big wedding. I just need to be married to you."

"It's too late now. Invitations are sent. Along with emails and calls made to let everyone know the venue is changed. Susan said she'd have someone at the inn let people know to go to Magic Cafe if they show up at the inn. Besides, Susan and Tally would kill me if we eloped. Tally has worked so hard to pull the wedding off at Magic Cafe with just a couple weeks' notice." Julie rubbed her temple, then forced a smile. She wanted Reed to have the kind of fancy wedding he was used to going to. The kind of wedding people in his world had, the kind he deserved. She wanted everything to be perfect, and she wanted him to be proud of her.

"I'm sure everything will be perfect. My friends will love you. How could they not?" He grinned at her, then got up and stood behind her chair. He started to rub her shoulders and some of the tension began to seep away.

"Um, that feels good." She tilted her head from side to side, working the kinks out. "You spoil me."

"You better get used to it." He leaned down and

pressed a kiss to her cheek. "Now you sit here and relax. I'm going to finish up the salad I made us for dinner."

"You really are the best."

"Don't you forget it." He winked at her and headed inside.

Reed looked back to make sure Julie wasn't following him. She'd leaned back in her chair and closed her eyes. He hoped he'd chased away at least part of her worries. He'd love to help with expenses at The Sweet Shoppe, but she'd never let him. He understood how she wanted her bakery to be all hers, and he admired her for that. It was one of the many reasons he'd fallen in love with her. That, and the fact that she'd saved him from himself and the cold, lonely life he thought was his for eternity.

But he did know just what he was going to give her for a wedding present. Well, okay, he'd already given her this beach house, but, sue him, he loved to spoil her.

He had one more present in mind. It was just what she wanted. What she needed. Even if she didn't know it.

He loved the woman with his whole heart and

would do anything for her. Anything. He was so lucky he'd found her and had a second chance at love. It was way more than he deserved.

Sure of himself, he picked up the phone to call his assistant in Seattle. She was a miracle worker as far as he was concerned and would know just how to do this. After talking to his assistant, he called Tally and told her his plan. Tally agreed it was a perfect idea.

With the Tally seal of approval, he knew he'd made a good choice.

CHAPTER 12

Tally was crazy busy at the cafe making sure everything was ready for the wedding. She shouldn't have said yes, but when Eddie asked if he could come over to her house later tonight after the dinner rush, she'd agreed. He said he'd gotten the photos scanned, and he'd return the album.

She hurried home about nine and found him sitting on her front step, waiting for her. He smiled and stood when he saw her. "I was a bit early, but it was a nice night to just sit."

Tally looked up at the stars twinkling in the sky. It was a pretty night, the kind the island was known for this time of year. The night air was still, and the moon was approaching full moon stage, shining silvery light down upon the island. She did dearly love this island.

She climbed the stairs and opened the door. "Come on in."

Eddie came in and handed the album to her. "Here. I appreciate you letting me borrow it."

"You got everything you wanted?"

"I… well, I scanned them all." Eddie shrugged sheepishly. "Couldn't help myself."

"There are more. We'll look through them and you can scan any you want."

"I'd appreciate that."

Tally swallowed and screwed up her courage. Sometimes it helped to just face your fears and get it over with. "You want to go see his room? It's… well, I haven't changed anything in it. I just… never could."

"I would like that." Unmistakable eagerness shone in his eyes.

They climbed the stairs, Eddie's heavy footsteps echoing in the stairway. Tally paused in front of Jackson's room, her hand resting on the doorknob. She took a deep breath. "It's this one." She pushed open the door and stood back for Eddie to enter.

Eddie took in every inch of his son's room. The stale air from being closed up. A poster of a band on one wall and a poster of a baseball player on another. A long shelf full of trophies. He crossed over and picked up one of them, wondering how many times his son had picked up this very same trophy to look at it. How many times had his son's hands touched the very spot where he held it? He held the trophy against his chest, then set it carefully back on the shelf.

Tally sat on the desk chair, silent, and let him explore. He picked up the baseball bat in the corner, running his hand along it, wrapping his fingers around it. The same grip his son would have had. His heart beat in a tripping rhythm, and he took a deep breath to steady his nerves.

Tally popped up and crossed over to the window, staring outside, but Eddie didn't think she was really seeing anything in the darkness out the window. She then turned and crossed back to sit on the bed. Within a minute, she was up and back by the window.

He crossed over to the desk and picked up a notebook sitting on it. Something slipped out and fluttered to the floor. He bent over to pick up a handful of photographs.

Tally walked over and peeked over his

shoulder. A frown crossed her face as she reached for one of them. "That's Jackson at college. I can see his dorm in the background. But I don't know who this is." She pointed to the blonde girl in the photo.

"He's got his arm around her. I wonder if she was someone he was dating?"

Tally's forehead creased. "I… I don't know. He didn't say anything to me. But then, he'd only been home from college one day when…" Her voice trailed off.

Eddie flipped the photos over, hoping to see something written on the back. A name. Something. But the reverse side just had the year stamped on them.

Tally peered at the back of the photo she was holding. "That was the last year he was… here. I wonder who she was."

Eddie rifled through the notebook to see if any more photos were stuffed in it. "That's all of them."

"She didn't come looking for him after he was gone. If she was his girlfriend or a good friend of his, she would have wondered where he was and tried to find him, right?" Tally trailed a finger over the image of her son in the photograph. "I guess we'll never know."

They'd probably never know. Eddie's heart

clutched in his chest. There was *so much* he'd never know about his son.

~

Long after Eddie left, Tally sat on the couch, holding the photographs they'd found. She held one under the light and looked at it once again. The pretty blonde girl was laughing, and Jackson's face was covered in a big goofy grin. He looked completely happy and at ease.

Who was she? She certainly looked the part of a girlfriend, but Jackson hadn't said a word about her. Maybe they broke up right before he came home for the summer? But he hadn't seemed upset when he came home. As she remembered, he'd seemed happy. More than happy.

But then why hadn't the girl come looking for him?

She sorted through the photos, looking at them one by one, searching for a clue. So strange to see a snippet of Jackson's life that she'd had no knowledge of, a glimpse of his life she wasn't a part of.

Then her heart caught, and a thought struck her with the full force of a hurricane. She dropped the photos onto the coffee table.

Eddie. He must feel just like this. He must feel

like this about Jackson's *entire life*. She could only show him glimpses of it from old photographs and from telling him stories. He could only grasp the fleeting moments she'd captured with the camera or the stories of Jackson that were flooding back into her consciousness.

Eddie had missed so much, and she felt responsible for that. If only she would have left with him when he asked her all those years ago. Eddie would have known his son, and Jackson would never have lived here on Belle Island by the ocean. He would have been tucked safely in the middle of Texas. Okay, not exactly the middle, but inland and away from the murderous sea.

Tally looked around the room. The room that hadn't changed in over twenty years. Faded couch, worn area rug on the old weathered floorboards, yellowed lampshade on a lamp that had been in that very spot since she'd been a little girl.

Tally rubbed her face, suddenly overtired and close to tears. She couldn't deal with the out-of-control feeling these last few days. She slowly pushed off the couch, feeling older than she'd ever allowed herself to feel before.

CHAPTER 13

"Come, take a walk with me." The next day Eddie stood on the steps to Magic Cafe. "I waited for the lull between breakfast and lunch."

"Oh, Eddie. I have so much to do." Tally shook her head.

Tereza looked up from cleaning the table next to them. "You should go. You look like you could use a break. I'll be here and Courtney should be here within a half hour. I've got this."

"Are you sure?" Tally didn't look convinced.

Eddie reached out his hand. "Come on. Come play hooky for just a little bit."

"Well, I can't argue with both of you." Tally set down a pitcher of water. "But not for long. I need to be back before the lunch crowd."

"You'll be back. I swear." Eddie crossed his heart and Tally laughed.

"Let's go then." She kicked off her shoes. "Here, leave your shoes with mine."

Eddie slipped off his shoes, the welcoming sand wrapping around his feet. A few fluffy white clouds floated across the sky. The spring sunshine bathed them with gentle warmth. They fell into step and crossed the sand to the shoreline. Tally stood at the edge and let the waves wash over her bare feet. The breeze tossed her hair around her face, just like it had so many years ago, only now it was laced with gray. The face looked so much the same, and yet so different. She turned and caught him staring at her and smiled.

"So, which way?" He looked up and down the beach.

"This way." She pointed.

They started walking slowly along the shore. Tally paused every so often to pick up a shell.

He laughed. "Still a shell collector, I see?"

"I can't help myself. They are always calling to me. It's not like I don't have thousands of shells in every imaginable container at home. There are some shells that still insist I pick them up." She grinned sheepishly.

"I would expect no less of you."

They came to an outcropping of land with a handful of large rocks jutting out into the sea. "Want to sit for a bit?" Tally pointed to the rocks.

"Sure." They climbed up on the rocks and settled down facing the ocean.

Tally shielded her eyes to watch a blue heron slowly, methodically flap its way down the shore. Once the bird was in the distance, she turned to him. "So, how about you tell me a bit about you? Do you still live in Texas?"

"I moved on from Texas years ago. I've lived all over. I've been in sales. Lots of sales. I think I could sell anything." Almost anything. He hadn't been able to sell Tally on coming with him when he'd left Belle Island all those years ago.

He pushed the thoughts away and continued talking about himself like Tally had requested. "I lived out of Los Angeles, a brief stint in San Francisco, a handful of years in Kentucky. Oh, and Chicago and Memphis."

"Wow, you've moved all over."

"And you never left Belle Island?"

"No. Stayed here the whole time."

"Well, you have a lot of family history here. Generations and generations of your family lived here."

Tally gazed out at the horizon. "But I'm the last

Belle. I thought Jackson would carry on the family line, but it wasn't meant to be. Since I was an only child, too... well, the Belle line is finished with me."

Eddie couldn't imagine having a family legacy like Tally did. He'd never met his biological father, and his mother's family was long gone. His stepfather had included him in his family though. Families were funny things. Sometimes you were born into them, sometimes they just kind of seemed to choose you.

"I'm sorry there won't be any more Belles on the island. That just seems... strange." Eddie glanced over at Tally.

"Well, it is what it is," she said in her typical matter-of-fact way. The one that hid how she really felt.

They sat in comfortable silence, listening to the waves splash and the birds call to each other.

Finally she turned to him. "So, do you have to get back to work soon?"

"Soon. I've been doing some while I'm here. I have my laptop and cell phone. I can do a lot of my job as long as I have those two things."

"What are you selling now?"

"Industrial adhesive."

"Like... *glue*?" Tally eyed him quizzically.

He laughed. "Not exactly. More heavy duty than that. You'd be surprised at the market for industrial adhesive and the companies that need it."

"If you say so." She grinned.

"What else do you want to know?" He rested his arms on his knees, enjoying the easy banter.

"Do you have family?"

"My mom and stepfather still live in Texas. I try to go see them as often as possible."

Tally's eyes held the briefest flash of jealousy, but she hid it quickly. "Did you ever marry?"

"Nope. Never did." All these years and the women he dated had never measured up to the girl he'd fallen in love with so long ago. The one who had refused to come with him when he moved from the island.

The one he'd left behind.

Tally sat silently next to Eddie. The sunshine warmed her in the way it had of thawing a person all the way to their bones after a long hard winter. She stretched her arms out in front of her and let the sun bake its magic.

Eddie was just inches away from her, his chest rising and falling with each breath. His hand rested on the rock beside her, less than an inch away.

For a moment she was back in time. Back when they'd been dating. Back when he'd been her whole world. She'd been madly in love with him. Everything about him. His smile. His laugh. His eyes. The way he held her tight and whispered in her ear, murmurs that were only meant for her.

"What are you thinking about?" Eddie's voice broke into her thoughts.

"I… I was thinking about things. How things were long ago. When we were kids."

"I was nuts about you back then. You know that, don't you?" His voice was low and swelled with emotion.

"I… cared… about you too."

"I never told you I loved you back then. I was too afraid. Afraid of rejection. Afraid you didn't feel the same way." His eyes clouded.

Eddie's words made her catch her breath. Did that mean he *had* loved her back then? She hadn't been sure. He'd never said it.

"I was a foolish kid, with too much pride. And a coward. I should have said it, told you I loved you. Maybe then you would have come with me."

Tally shook her head. "I think even if you'd told me how you felt back then, I'd still have stayed on the island. I couldn't see myself leaving my father here all alone."

Eddie sighed. "I know. I think we were just in the wrong place at the wrong time in our lives."

"Maybe."

He reached over and touched her face, his warm hand scalding a trail across her cheek. She reached up to cover his hand and pressed it close.

"You know, I never forgot you." He looked into her eyes. "Oh, I tried to. I really did. But I couldn't erase my memory of you. The way you felt in my arms. The way…" He hesitantly leaned over, paused, then kissed her gently on her lips.

Her heart cartwheeled as she kissed him back, her mind a twirling vortex of thoughts.

He slowly pulled away. "I never forgot the way it felt to kiss you."

She placed a finger against her lips, so empty now that he'd stopped kissing her. "Eddie… I…"

"It's okay. You don't need to say anything." Eddie reached over and pulled her against him, tucking her safely against him.

It was a good thing he didn't need her to talk because she was fairly certain she'd never be able to describe how she felt this very minute, much less utter a coherent word.

CHAPTER 14

Courtney walked out on the deck at Magic Cafe, tying on her server apron as she crossed the worn planks. "Hey, Tereza."

"Oh, glad you're here. We got a large, early group for lunch and Tally is out taking a walk." Tereza balanced a tray on one hip and carried a pitcher of tea in her other hand.

"Tally is out taking a walk?" Courtney hadn't known Tally very long, but she didn't seem like the type of person to just take a walk as the lunch crowd was gathering.

"Yep. I told her it would do her good. She's out with her new friend, that Eddie guy."

"Well, tell me where to start." Courtney glanced around at the crowd.

"Take table four and catch the next table that gets seated."

"Will do." Courtney put on a smile and headed over to get table four's order. She chatted with the people, trying to sound as friendly as Tereza. But Tereza's banter sounded so genuine, and Courtney felt like hers was forced. She'd have to learn to do better. She wanted Tally to be proud of the way she did her job. It was the least she could do in return for everything Tally had done for her.

The hostess sat another table and Courtney hurried over to get the man's order. She looked down at him as she approached the table and froze. Sheriff Dave. She looked quickly for Tereza, but she was busy waiting on another table. Sheriff Dave looked up at her and her skin tingled. She swallowed.

"Hi, are you ready to order?"

"Well, hello again. You're that new waitress Tally hired, aren't you? I think Tally said your name is Courtney?"

She nodded. Why hadn't she thought to change her name? Well, that wouldn't have worked because she needed identification to cash her paycheck and… it was all so complicated.

"I'll have a sweet tea for now. Give me a minute to figure out what I want to eat."

"Sure." Courtney turned and fled, feeling the sheriff's eyes on her back, burning into her.

Or maybe she imagined it.

Or maybe she hadn't.

Tereza cornered her in the kitchen. "Okay, something is going on. I know it. When Sheriff Dave comes in, you turn as pale as a bleached-out sand dollar. Is there some reason you want to avoid him?"

Courtney fought back the fear that threatened to overwhelm her. "I…"

"Okay, look. I'll take his table. But after lunch, when it's not busy, you're going to talk to me. Got it?" Tereza commanded in a no-nonsense voice. "Just maybe, I can help you."

"I don't think anyone can help me." Courtney's voice trailed off.

Tally hurried onto the deck at the restaurant, trying to collect her thoughts. The lunch crowd was in full swing. She should have been back here half an hour ago. She stopped by a table to say hi to Paul and Josephine. Her friend was all smiles and held his wife's hand in his. It was clear to see all was right with his world.

"You okay, Tally? You look all flushed." Paul questioned her.

"I'm fine. Just a bit of heat from the sunshine."

Paul didn't look like he believed her, but she smiled and quickly walked back into the kitchen.

"Tereza, I'm sorry I took so long."

"No problem. Everything is fine."

The restaurant was bustling, but it really did look like Tereza had things under control, in the crazy busy way they got sometimes.

"Hand me that tray you have. What table is it going to?"

"Table three. Sheriff Dave."

"Got it." Tally pushed back out onto the deck and crossed over to the sheriff's table with his fried grouper sandwich.

"Hi, Dave. Good to see you."

Sheriff Dave looked up. "Hey, Tally."

She set his food on the table.

"That new waitress of yours? Courtney? Do you know where she's from?" Sheriff Dave's face was creased in thought.

"All over, I think."

"So she's brand new to the island?"

"Yes."

"She's got a kid that Dorothy's niece is watching?"

"Yep."

"Hm."

Tally wanted to ask why he had so many questions, but another large group of customers came in, so she hurried off to seat them.

She couldn't stop the nagging feeling that arose from his questions. Courtney was a skittish thing. An unexpected sense of overprotectiveness crept over her.

Tereza and Courtney sat on the small deck outside the storage building after they finished their shift. Courtney had tried to escape unnoticed, but Tereza had nailed her with a wait-a-minute glare.

"Now, why don't you tell me what's going on." Tereza swayed slowly back and forth on the rocker.

"Nothing's going on."

"Don't ever play poker. You'll lose." Tereza shot her a wry grin.

"I… I just need to not be found for a while."

"You in trouble with the law?"

"Not exactly. I don't think so." She sighed. "Well, maybe. To be honest, I didn't stay around long enough to find out."

Tereza frowned. "Tally doesn't need any trouble."

"Oh, I know. She's been so kind. Bobby and I should probably just leave."

"Now, I didn't say that." Tereza leaned forward. "You didn't kill someone, or rob somebody, or some felony like that, right?"

Courtney gave her new friend a weak smile. "No, nothing like that." Though, kidnapping was probably a felony…

"You going to tell me what's going on?"

Courtney shoved her hair behind her ear. "I… all I feel comfortable saying is that there is someone who… who I don't want to find me."

"Or find Bobby?" Tereza raised an eyebrow.

"Or find Bobby." Her pulse raced. Especially find Bobby.

Tereza reached over and squeezed her hand. "Okay, then. If you don't want to be found, we'll make sure you aren't found. I'm sure you have a good reason."

Courtney didn't know if she felt better or worse for telling Tereza that tiny bit of truth.

CHAPTER 15

Mary and Tally strolled down the beach with Stormy and Bobby. The boy and puppy ran up and down the beach in front of them but never got far. Courtney had warned him before they left that he needed to stay close.

"Bobby sure loves that pup of yours." Tally laughed when Bobby got tangled up in the leash and spun in circles to unwind.

"Stormy has brought a lot of joy to my life. Makes me focus on something else than… well, than my disease. He makes me just appreciate all the little extraordinary moments I do have now." Mary put a hand above her eyes and shielded her view from the sun.

"Mary, you have a remarkable attitude. I admire

you so much. You are very brave." Tally studied the woman beside her.

"Oh, I'm not brave. Sometimes I'm scared to death of what's happening. But, I just take it one day at a time. Enjoy what I have."

"I still think you're one of the bravest people I know." Tally watched as Bobby threw a stick and then he and Stormy raced to get it.

Tally watched as Bobby and Stormy plowed into Camille Montgomery. Camille went down with a thud. "Uh, oh."

Tally and Mary hurried up to her. "Are you okay, Camille?" She offered the woman her hand.

"I am *not* okay. Who let this boy and this beast run loose on the beach with no supervision?" Camille snapped.

Tally took her hand back. Camille could crawl up by herself. "They were playing. And we were watching them."

"I'm sorry lady. I got tangled up in the leash. That *always* happens when I walk Stormy."

Delbert Hamilton hurried across the sandy expanse in front of Camille's beach house. "Are you okay, hon? You took quite a tumble." He reached down and effortlessly pulled Camille to her feet.

Camille's carefully pressed slacks had a streak of dirt on them. She swiped at it ineffectually. "No,

I'm not okay. This is outrageous. A person should be able to walk on their own beach without being attacked."

"I'm not sure this qualifies as an attack." Delbert grinned at Bobby. "I think it was more of an accident."

"It was. I didn't mean to knock the lady down. I told her I was sorry… but she didn't say it was okay… I think she's mad at me."

"Camille, tell the boy you're fine."

"I'm not fine. Look at these slacks."

"I'm sure the dry cleaners can get that stain out." Delbert turned back to Bobby. "So, have you found any more starfish?"

"Nope. Not a one. Momma says there are some at the point though. We're gonna go look there when she has time off from work. She works all the time."

"Grownups do that," Delbert said gravely.

"That's no fun."

"I guess it depends on whether you like your job or not."

Camille brushed more sand from her slacks. "Well, I'm going in to change. It's a good thing we're going to rent this house if this is what it's like on the beach now."

Camille spun around and stalked across the

beach toward her house. She lost her balance at one point but caught herself before she went down again.

"Don't worry about her. She'll be fine." Delbert ruffled Bobby's hair. "You just keep walking that pup and tire him out."

"I don't think Stormy ever tires out." With that, Bobby went racing down to the waves. He came dashing back a moment later. "Will you tell that lady I'm sorry again?"

"I will, son."

Bobby smiled in relief and rushed back toward the water with Stormy at his side.

"I hope Camille is okay." Tally did hope she was okay even if she was perturbed at how Camille had spoken to Bobby. You'd think the woman had never had a speck of dirt on her clothing before.

"I'm sure she's fine, but I better go in and check on her." Mr. Hamilton turned and started up toward the house.

"That Camille needs a lesson in manners." Mary shook her head. "Bobby was just being a boy. And he apologized. She could have accepted his apology."

"That's just Camille being Camille." Tally turned and locked arms with Mary. "Let's head back before it gets too late."

Later that day Tally stood at the edge of the sand, watching Courtney romp around the beach with Bobby. He'd created some elaborate game involving pirates and aliens as far as Tally could tell. Courtney was playing along as commanded by the boy. She waved a palm frond to hold off the imaginary pirates. A smile tugged at the corners of Tally's mouth as she watched the scene.

Eddie came walking up the beach and lifted a hand in a wave. Tally wasn't sure she liked the way her heart fluttered when he simply walked into her view. She wasn't that young school girl anymore. She was a grown woman for goodness' sake.

Eddie came and stood beside her, looking at her like he was taking in a long swig of a much-needed drink. Without saying a word, he placed his hand on hers resting on the railing.

Her heart did another traitorous flip in her chest.

Courtney glanced up from their game and waved. Bobby looked up and called out. "Hey, Miss Tally, come play. You can be a space guy or a pirate."

"I bet you've always wanted to be a pirate." Eddie winked at her.

"Always." Tally slipped her hand out from under his—reluctantly—and crossed down to the sand. She was aware of Eddie just steps behind her. She walked up to Courtney and Bobby and introduced Eddie to them. "Courtney, Bobby, this is Eddie —Edward."

"Eddie is fine. Nice to meet both of you." He turned to Bobby. "So, young man, if Miss Tally here gets to be a pirate, what do I get to be?"

Bobby screwed up his face and looked at Eddie carefully, eyeing him up and down. "I *think* you might be okay for the space guy. He's a good guy. The pirates are bad guys."

"Well, thank you. I've always thought I was the good guy kind of man." Eddie winked at Tally and crossed over to where Bobby told him to hide in the spaceship. The spaceship that looked amazingly like a couple of lounge chairs flipped on their side.

They all played Bobby's elaborate game until Courtney dropped to the sand in exhaustion. "You win, Bobby."

The boy strutted up to them. "I'm always the good guy. I always win."

"It's nice for the good guys to win." Tally sank onto the sand beside Courtney. She leaned closer to the girl. "I think good guys have more energy than bad guys."

Courtney laughed. "I think they do."

Bobby raced down toward the waves and Eddie jogged after him. They both started running back and forth, letting the waves chase them up the beach. Eddie picked up Bobby, swung him high, and pretended like he was going to toss him into the ocean. Bobby shrieked with laughter. When Eddie put him down, Bobby raced down the beach.

"Bobby, that's too far." Courtney jumped up and started after him.

Eddie waved to her and headed after the boy, motioning him to come back. Eddie met him halfway and they paused, looking at something on the sand.

"Looks like Bobby found a new friend." Courtney settled back down next to Tally.

"It appears so. Not sure which of them is having the better time." Tally watched as Eddie talked to Bobby, then pointed out to sea. Eddie was really good with Bobby. She sat watching the two of them interact.

An inescapable sadness crept over her. Eddie hadn't ever had the chance to do simple things like play on the beach with his own son. He had missed so much.

Courtney waited for her pulse to settle. She'd had a momentary panic when Bobby raced down the beach. She hoped Tally hadn't noticed her fright. Would she ever be okay when Bobby was out of her sight? She had a hard enough time leaving him with Belinda, but she needed to earn money so she had no choice. How had she managed to get herself, and Bobby, into this mess? She'd been a fool about Kurt, that was for sure. A mistake she'd never make again.

She watched as Eddie played with her son. Bobby was having so much fun. He was getting so much attention on Belle Island, and he was thriving under it all. Guilt washed over her that it would soon all be taken away from him. He'd lost so much in his young life. He was used to no continuity at all.

She hoped she'd managed to let him know he was loved and wanted, but she hadn't been able to give him a stable home. She'd wanted that so badly for him. But she'd failed.

Six months ago she'd let down her guard when she thought she'd finally located them a safe place to stay, but they'd been found and soon were on the run again. She didn't plan on making that mistake again. She wasn't going to be lulled into a false security here on the island.

She rubbed the back of her neck and watched

while Eddie and Bobby tossed shells into the sea. A bone-weary tiredness soaked through her. It was all so exhausting, and she worried about the toll it was taking on Bobby.

She just wanted to keep him safe and provide him some stability in life. Was that too much for a mother to ask?

Eddie dropped onto the sand beside Tally when Courtney finally took Bobby inside. "The kid is amazing. Sharp boy. But wow, does he have a lot of energy."

Tally laughed. "Apparently, so do you."

"It's not every day a person gets to be a space guy." He grinned. "Or a pirate."

"Bobby certainly isn't lacking in imagination." Tally picked up a handful of sand and let it sift through her fingers. She glanced at her watch. "I'd better go. Need to get ready for the dinner crowd and I still have a lot to do for Julie's wedding."

"Julie's wedding?" Eddie had no idea who Julie was.

"Julie's a friend of mine. She was supposed to have her wedding at the inn, but they had a fire and their kitchen is closed."

"Yes, they told me about the fire when I checked into the inn."

"Anyway, I offered to have it here at Magic Cafe. We're going to have the ceremony out here on the beach, then a reception out on the deck. I'm closing the restaurant for the evening."

"Can I do anything to help? I feel kind of at loose ends here and I'd love something to keep me busy."

"I thought you were working while you were here?" Tally looked at him.

"I am, but things are kind of slow right now."

"You don't have to help." She shook her head.

"But I *want* to."

"Okay then, how do you feel about taking the van over to the inn and picking up the chairs? Susan is loaning them to me."

"I could do that." Eddie was happy to help, and it was an excuse to keep seeing Tally. He couldn't get the memory of that kiss out of his mind, and he'd tried. He'd lain in bed last night, staring at the ceiling, unable to sleep, reliving the kiss and wondering why he hadn't thought to kiss her again.

Enough of that. He shook his head to clear his thoughts and stood up, reaching out a hand for hers. She slipped her hand in his, and he effortlessly lifted her to her feet. He steadied her for a moment before she caught her balance. She smiled at him as she brushed the sand from her pants.

"I do appreciate the help with the wedding preparations. Let me go get you the keys. I'll call Susan and tell her you're coming."

He followed her into Magic Cafe, watching as she gracefully crossed the sand and climbed the steps to the deck. She looked at home here at the cafe, confident she was in the right place where she belonged. He couldn't imagine living in one place for his whole life. A place where he belonged and felt a part of. His nomad life had never allowed him that... luxury. He *did* consider it a luxury. A luxury that suddenly, unexpectedly, he felt was missing from his life.

CHAPTER 16

Eddie unloaded the chairs into the storage building to store them until the wedding. He carried armload after armload of white wooden chairs inside and set them against the wall. After he finished, he went off to look for Tally.

He found her busy with the dinner crowd.

"Eddie, thanks for your help. Let me repay you by at least giving you a nice meal. Why don't you take that table over at the edge of the beach?"

He wasn't going to say no to dinner, and his stomach growled in agreement to his decision. "Sounds good. Can you join me for a bit?"

Tally looked around the restaurant. "It's pretty busy right now. Maybe in a little bit. I'll send Tereza over to take your order."

The waitress who had told him where to find Tally the first day he'd come to town walked up to his table with a friendly smile. "Hi, I'm Tereza. Tally wanted me to get you anything you want from the menu. Do you want to start with a cold drink?"

"Hey, Tereza. I'm Eddie." He paused. He'd introduced himself as Eddie, not Edward. How long had it been since he'd done that?

"Nice to meet you, Eddie. Tally said you're a friend of hers."

A friend. Well, he guessed that about covered it. Probably. A friend and so much more... and yet, not. He chased his flitting thoughts away. "I'll take a Corona and lime."

"You've got it."

Tereza walked away, and Eddie settled back in his chair. He waved to Courtney across the room. She was busy waiting on a table by the door. He watched Tally greet a group of customers and seat them at a table. She walked past another table and stopped to talk to the couple for a few minutes. She grabbed a tray and cleared a table, then came walking out of the back room—the kitchen, he'd guess—with a full tray of food and delivered it to another table. She seemed to be everywhere at once with a proficient, graceful ease.

She looked his direction once and smiled at

him. He smiled back, glad to just be around her, even if she was busy working. Tereza came back with his beer and he delayed ordering, hoping to persuade Tally to join him.

Tally walked by later and stopped at his table. "You don't have your meal yet?"

"I was waiting to order. Hoping you'd have dinner with me."

She looked around the restaurant. "I could do that. Things are slowing down. I might have to jump up if I'm needed though."

"I'm okay with that." He was okay with anything if she'd just sit down across from him and spend time with him.

She walked over and spoke to Tereza, returned to the table, and sank into the chair across from him. "I'm going to have a beer with you."

He grinned at her. "Good for you. Way to be a rebel."

"Hey, I own the place. I should be able to take a break and have a drink with an old friend."

*Friend.* There was that word again.

Tally sat across from Eddie while he ate his dinner. She'd just ordered a salad, but he'd gotten a salad, an appetizer, and the catch of the day, blackened. She enjoyed watching him relish each bite.

She tried not to stare. Not to stare at his strong hands. Not to stare at his face with the beginning of a tan and a hint of sunburn. Not to stare at his eyes that glimmered when he laughed. Or his lips. She definitely didn't stare at his lips while he sipped his beer. Or think about what it had been like to kiss him again after all these years.

"You're staring at me." Eddie grinned at her.

"I am not."

"Okay, whatever you say." He shrugged, but a self-satisfied smile tugged at the corners of his mouth.

"Okay, maybe I was." She set her beer on the table. "But it feels so… surreal… to have you back here on Belle Island. I thought I'd never see you again, that the fates didn't want me to find you."

"Ah, but then they did."

"Only… it was too late." Her voice dropped.

He reached out and covered her hand with his. "No, it's not too late. I'm glad I came back. I am sorry I missed Jackson's life, but I'm grateful to hear about it. I'm glad I found out I had a son. Grateful to see the photos. And…" He set down his fork. "I'm really grateful to have found you again, Tally."

She didn't know what to say to that. She was

enjoying her time with him. And much like Susan had predicted, it was helping to talk about Jackson again. The pain was still there, but it was being wrapped up with wonderful memories of the good times.

"Your face looks… I don't know… sad and yet, not sad." Eddie's eyes were filled with puzzlement in their depths. "I used to be able to know what you were thinking, just by looking at you."

"Well, I've had a few years to learn how to hide my thoughts."

"You don't have to hide them from me."

She looked at him, wanting to believe him, but it had been so long that she'd kept her feelings to herself. Protected herself. It was easier that way.

Besides, deep inside, she truly believed she didn't deserve more than her simple life now. She'd made mistakes. Mistakes that had cost her dearly. And Eddie was a complication. Besides, he'd be leaving soon. She didn't want to feel anything about him because he'd leave and there would be that empty hole in her life again. She wasn't sure she could do that again, live with the void of someone leaving her.

She stood up abruptly. "I should go. I have chores to do to close up the restaurant and still have things to do for Julie's wedding. It's in two days. So much to do."

"Tally, don't go. Don't run away."

"I'm not running. I'm just busy."

Eddie let out a long whoosh of air. "I'm sticking around for a while, Tally. I'm not going anywhere. We're going to sit down and talk. Talk about what this is."

"There's nothing to talk about. You're leaving. Yesterday's kiss was just a momentary slip into the past. A mistake." She started to walk away, but Eddie gently caught her wrist and stopped her.

"It was more than that," he insisted.

"It can't be." Tally pulled away and hurried off to the safety of her office.

Eddie watched Tally rush away from the table, no longer looking the confident I-belong-here-woman. She looked more like she wanted to be anywhere on earth but here. Running away. Running away *from him*. He'd wanted to stop her, but when Tally made up her mind, there wasn't much chance of changing it. He remembered that fact well enough. He hadn't been able to convince her to come with him all those years ago, and he wasn't sure he'd be able to…

*To what?*

What was it he wanted?

He picked up his beer and took a long swallow of the cool liquid. It did little to quench his thirst or the thrumming of his pulse.

One thing was certain—Tally could twist his thoughts up into knots. She'd always done that to him and it appeared the years hadn't lessened her ability.

He stared in the direction she'd disappeared. He set his beer down with a clatter and jumped up from the table. With determined strides, he went off in the direction she had disappeared.

When he found her office, he peeked through the half-opened door. Tally sat at her desk, the low light of a lamp illuminating her face. She stared into space, lost in thought. He rapped on the door frame and she looked up, startled.

Three long strides and he reached her desk. He extended his hands and pulled her to her feet. His pulse raced when a small gasp escaped her. He gently reached down and tilted her chin up, then lowered his lips to hers. Her hand grasped the front of his shirt, bunching it tightly as she responded to his kiss.

He finally pulled his lips away, but tucked her up against his chest, savoring the closeness, feeling her heart beat with his. He could stand like this forever and die a contented man.

"We can't do this, Eddie." Her words were muffled against him. She pulled back and looked directly into his eyes. "*I* can't do this."

In an instant, his contentment was shattered.

"Yes. Yes, you can. *We* can." He let her go and took a step back. "We're not done. There is still so much unfinished between us." He reached out and trailed a finger along her cheek.

"You have to let this go."

"We don't even know what *this* is yet. But you can't deny there is something between us. Still."

She shook her head slowly back and forth, a sad expression on her face.

He tried to reach for her again, but she took a step back.

He slowly turned away and left her office, his heart hammering in his chest and his lips burning from her kiss.

CHAPTER 17

The next morning Tally stood by the door of the storage building chatting with Courtney while Bobby played with some hero figures in the sand beside them. The boy had the most vivid imagination.

Susan hurried up to them, her eyes clouded with concern. "Have you seen Mary's puppy, Stormy? He got away from her this morning. She's so worried."

Bobby jumped up, his eyes bright. "Stormy ran away?"

"I'm sure we'll find him," Susan assured him but her eyes belied her confidence.

Bobby tugged on Courtney's hand. "Momma, let's help find him."

"Bobby, we need to go inside and get cleaned up. It's time for you to go to Miss Belinda's and I have to work."

"But Momma." A thunderous look swept across Bobby's face.

"Don't worry, Bobby. We'll find him. My son is out looking with Mary, too." Susan patted Bobby's shoulder.

"But I wanna help. Stormy's probably scared."

"I'm sure they'll let us know when he's found." Courtney took Bobby's hand, and he kicked the sand to let his mother know his displeasure. "Bobby." Courtney's voice held a warning note.

He looked contrite and followed his mother inside.

"I could help you look." Tally frowned. "I bet Mary is upset. She's really grown attached to that little dog."

Susan nodded. "She is. But it's almost time for the lunch crowd here at Magic Cafe. You go ahead and work. I know you're crazy busy with finishing up the wedding things and your regular workload. After we find Stormy, I still plan on coming over this afternoon and helping with the centerpieces for the tables."

"You go on then and look for the pup. Good luck."

"Thanks, Tally." Susan turned and hurried down the beach.

Tally hoped they would find Stormy. The pup brought so much joy to the tough stage of life Mary was at now. The woman deserved all the happiness she could get.

Courtney finished changing into clothes for work and walked out of the bathroom. "Bobby, you ready to go?"

She looked around the small room. Bobby was nowhere to be seen. He must be waiting for her out on the front deck. She took a quick look in the mirror, then glanced down at her feet. She really should consider a new pair of more comfortable shoes. But then, that was money she couldn't save, so... no new shoes.

She opened the door and stepped outside. Bobby wasn't on the stoop. She looked out at the beach in front of the building, though he knew he wasn't allowed on the beach without her. Panic began to race through her. How long had she been in the bathroom changing clothes? Enough time for Kurt to sneak in and find Bobby?

She hurried out onto the beach and looked both

ways, calling his name. The wind buffeted her calls. Her heart pounded as she put a hand up to shield her eyes from the glare of the sun and swept her gaze along the shore.

Maybe he'd gone over to Magic Cafe. She twirled around, hurried over to the restaurant, and bounded up the stairs to the deck. Tally was setting a tabletop and Courtney hurried over to her. "Have you seen Bobby?"

Tally looked up. "No, not since you went inside."

"I can't find him." Just saying the words out loud almost brought her to her knees. "I've looked. He's not in the building. I can't see him on the beach. I… I don't know where he could be." Her words choked in her throat.

Tally frowned. "You don't think he went off looking for Stormy, do you?"

Courtney paused and clutched the rung on the chair in front of her. That could be it. He *had* been angry with her when she said they didn't have time to help with the search. Bobby off looking for Stormy was preferable to Kurt finding him. But not by much.

"I know it's my shift soon, but I have to find him."

"And I'm going to help." Tally turned and

motioned to Tereza. "Bobby is missing. We're off looking for him. You got this? Call another waitress in if you need to."

"I will. You two don't worry about the cafe. Just go find Bobby." Tereza's eyes were filled with concern.

"You got your cell?" Tally reached and slid her phone from her pocket.

Courtney patted her back pocket. "Yes, it's here."

"What's going on?" Eddie walked up to them. "You both look a bit panicked."

"Bobby is missing." Courtney heard her voice shake.

"We think he went off looking for Stormy," Tally explained.

Eddie's face held a blank look.

"Stormy is Mary's dog. Mary is Susan's mother-in-law." Tally quickly filled him in. "Stormy got loose and we think Bobby went off to find him."

"Let me help." Eddie stepped forward.

"Okay. Here's what we'll do. Eddie, head toward the lighthouse. Courtney, head that way down the beach." Tally pointed in one direction. "I'm going to look around the cafe and the storage building and around the streets near here. I'll call Susan and have her keep an eye out for Bobby, too."

Courtney was grateful for someone taking charge. She had to find Bobby. What if he got too close to the ocean and got knocked over by a wave? Or got lost and scared? Or… she had to quit thinking like that.

"Hey, there's Sheriff Dave. I'll let him know Bobby is missing." Tally motioned the sheriff to come over.

Courtney's heart pounded in her chest, choking her breath. Her instinct was to run from the sheriff, but if he could help find Bobby…

"Dave, Courtney's son, Bobby, is missing. Can you call your guys and let them know in case anyone sees him?" Tally asked.

"Description?" Sheriff Dave took out a pad of paper.

Courtney shoved back her urge to run. "He's five. He has blonde hair. Curly, kinda. He was wearing…" Courtney frowned. What had he put on today? Why couldn't she remember? Her mind was a blank. What kind of mother didn't know what her son was wearing?

"He had on gray shorts and a red shirt," Tally filled in.

"Okay, I'll make some calls. I'll let you know if one of my men turn up anything."

"Thanks, Sheriff." Tally turned to Courtney. "Let's head out."

Courtney was more than ready to get away from the sheriff's prying eyes. She might be imagining it, but it seemed to her that he'd looked at her very peculiarly. She pushed the thought away. She'd deal with that later. Now it was all about finding Bobby.

Tereza gave Courtney a quick hug, her friendly arms providing strength. "We'll find him. It will be okay."

Courtney nodded, snagged her phone to look at it to make sure it had a good charge, and slipped it back in her pocket.

"Okay, call if anyone finds him." Tally took off through the cafe, and Courtney and Eddie headed toward the beach.

Courtney's heart pounded in her chest. Bobby had to be okay. He had to be.

She'd tried so hard to protect him. Protect him from his father. Not that Kurt should be allowed to call himself a father. But what if this wasn't Bobby out looking for Stormy? *What if Kurt had found Bobby?*

Eddie headed down the beach toward Lighthouse Point at a comfortable jog. He scanned the people on the beach and stopped occasionally to ask people if they'd seen Bobby. Unfamiliar thoughts crept through his mind. Worries about Bobby being hurt, lost, scared. He'd never had to look after a kid or be responsible for one. It must be huge and overwhelming to raise a kid, especially raising one on your own.

He rounded a curve on the beach, and a small tan and white puppy came running out of the bushes at the side of the beach. The pup stood, his tail raised high, and barked at Eddie. "Hey, little guy." He leaned down and scooped up the dog. "So, do you think your name is Stormy?"

The pup licked Eddie's face, and he grinned. He twisted the collar around to read the tag. "Stormy it is."

Eddie looked around in the direction Stormy had come, through the bushes lining the beach. "Well, one lost person—okay, dog—has been found. Now let's see if we can find Bobby."

The puppy barked. Eddie slipped off his belt and set the puppy down. He fastened the belt to Stormy's collar. "Let's go look by the lighthouse, Stormy." Eddie started back down the beach.

Stormy froze in place.

"Hey, come on. I have to keep looking for Bobby."

The dog refused to budge.

Eddie walked up to him. "Look, Bobby is missing. We have to go find him." *Why was he explaining all this to a dog?*

Stormy barked and lunged back toward the bushes. The belt slipped from Eddie's hand as the puppy darted forward. He frowned and sped after the puppy. He slipped through a small break in the bushes and came upon an old dilapidated gazebo in a grove of trees. Stormy stood by the gazebo and barked.

He was going to give that dog about one more minute before he was giving up on him and heading out to find Bobby. Someone else was going to have to chase after the silly pup.

Eddie crossed over slowly, trying not to scare the dog away. "Here, Stormy. Come here, pup. You know you want to," he cajoled the puppy.

"Mr. Eddie?" A small voice came from the gazebo.

Eddie crossed the distance in two long strides. "Bobby?" He looked down and saw Bobby splayed out on the rotted flooring of the gazebo, one leg hung down between two split planks of wood.

"So, what happened here?" Eddie took a step onto the gazebo and Bobby yelled.

"Ow. That's smashing my leg."

Eddie quickly assessed the situation. He didn't want to walk across the boards in case more of them were rotten.

"I fell through the floor. I can't get my foot out and there's blood." Tears trailed down the boys' cheek.

"I'll get you loose, son. Don't worry." Eddie eyed the boards. He could probably just pry a few boards up and reach him. "I'm going to pull up these two boards, then see if we can get your foot free."

Bobby nodded and swiped a dirty hand across his face.

Eddie reached down and pried up one board. The second board wasn't as cooperative, but he finally pried it loose, too. He used it to wrest off the board trapping Bobby, and suddenly the boy slid his leg out.

"I'm free. You saved me." Bobby's eyes glistened with tears.

Eddie scooped the boy up and carried him through the bushes. Bobby's small arms clung to his neck and Eddie hugged him close. He carried the boy out into the sunlight, set him down gently, and examined his leg.

"Got a bit of a cut there, but I think it will be okay." Eddie wasn't sure if it needed stitches or not, but he wasn't going to say that in front of the boy. "I'm going to wrap it in my shirt."

Eddie reached behind his neck, snatched his collar, and shucked his shirt. He gently wrapped it around Bobby's leg.

"My momma is going to kill me." Bobby's eyes were filled with tears. "I'm not supposed to go anywhere without an adult, but I was afraid Stormy was scared."

The darn dog. Where was he? Eddie spun around and saw Stormy sprawled out no more than a foot away, watching them.

"You shouldn't go places without an adult. That's a good rule." Eddie eyed the pup, making sure he was staying put.

"I'm going to call Tally and tell her I found you, then I'm going to bring you home."

Bobby sighed. "I hope it was good knowing me, 'cause Momma is going to ground me for *foooor-ever*."

Eddie smothered a smile. "Well, sometimes we have to take the consequences when we make mistakes."

Bobby let out another long sigh. "Yeah. I guess so."

"Your mom was really, really worried about you. Just like you were worried about Stormy."

"I didn't mean to worry her." Bobby's voice got low. "I shouldn't have. I know she's scared Kurt will find me."

"Who's Kurt?"

Bobby's eyes grew wide. "No one. I'm not supposed to talk about him. Don't tell Momma I said anything about him."

Eddie didn't want Bobby to get even more upset. "Okay. We won't talk about him." *What was that all about?*

Bobby's eyes filled with tears again.

"Don't cry." He was making things worse, not better. He had no experience with kids. None. Could he screw this up any more? "Come on. Let me bring you back to your mom."

Eddie called Tally on his cell, then scooped up the boy and the dog. He headed down the beach with Bobby held protectively against his chest and Stormy snuggled up in Bobby's arms.

How had he gotten to this point? He wasn't a family man, but here he was walking down the beach with a boy and a dog in his arms.

CHAPTER 18

"Bobby." Courtney ran up the beach toward Eddie and her son. She threw her arms around Bobby, Eddie, and Stormy in one exuberant hug. She kissed on Bobby and Stormy barked. They all laughed.

"Hi, Momma. Mr. Eddie found me." Her son scowled. "But you're mad at me, aren't you?"

"We'll talk about that later. Right now I'm just glad to have you back." She kissed him again, and he turned his head away.

"Aw, Momma, everyone is looking."

Tally came up and took Stormy into her arms. "Haven't you caused enough trouble for the day?" The dog licked her, and Tally laughed.

Courtney looked at Bobby's leg all wrapped up in a shirt and Eddie standing there shirtless. "What happened to Bobby's leg?" She frowned.

"He has a cut on it. I think it needs... attention." Eddie gave her a warning look.

"Set him here on this lounge chair and let me see it." She carefully unwrapped his leg and looked at the wound. "Well, buddy, I think we should have a doctor look at this."

"Really?" Bobby's lower lip trembled.

"We'll get it all fixed up." Courtney hugged her son, resisting—just barely—the urge to rain kisses down on him again.

Tally turned to Eddie. "Why don't you take Stormy? I called Susan, and she's on her way to pick him up. I'm going to take Courtney and Eddie to the doctor."

Courtney sighed. Another bill to contend with. But she was so grateful that Bobby was safe, if injured, that she figured it was worth it. She'd just work more hours... though that meant more time away from Bobby. She sighed.

"I'll carry Bobby to your car, then I'll take Stormy." Eddie scooped the boy up from the lounge chair.

"Thank you." Tally led the way and Courtney

was grateful for the ride. Her car was still in the shop, though the estimate for fixing it hadn't been as bad as she'd expected.

"I know you don't have your insurance card yet, but this should be covered. I have the info to give the doc."

"I have insurance already?" *How did she not know this?*

"Yep, I cover my workers from the day they start. It just takes a bit for the cards to come. Didn't I mention it?"

"That's… wonderful." Relief surged through Courtney. Finding Belle Island had been such a blessing.

Courtney sat on her bed after tucking Bobby in for the night. He'd had quite the day, complete with a few stitches in his leg. He'd been very brave about it, but it all had taken its toll on him. It took him all of about thirty seconds to fall asleep.

She was so grateful that things were working out. They had insurance for goodness' sake. And Tally was good about not scheduling her for the late shift, so she could pick Bobby up after the dinner rush was over. Belinda was agreeable to a flexible schedule. Things were almost working out too perfectly. But she wouldn't let herself believe in that fairy tale. She'd gotten too comfortable at their last stop, and look how that had turned out.

She'd just narrowly missed getting caught. But for a twist of fate where she happened to be looking out the window and spied Kurt's truck, everything would be different now. She'd grabbed Bobby, leaving most of their belongings behind, and rushed out the back way of the apartment building. She'd taken back roads away from town, then hidden out in the nearest big city for a few days. After that, they'd taken to the road again, driving mostly at night, until they'd ended up here on Belle Island.

When she'd seen the name of the town on the sign on the interstate, she'd immediately turned off and headed for it, not knowing why. But the town had a familiar ring to it. It had called her, and she'd obeyed.

Which had turned out to be a good decision.

At least for now.

Once she'd saved up a bit of money, they'd have to move on, of course. Bobby would be so disappointed, but it had to be. Maybe, eventually, Kurt would lose interest. She didn't even think he actually wanted Bobby, he just didn't want her to have him. Didn't want her to 'have' what he considered his property. And there was no way she was going to put Bobby in harm's way again. They could stay fugitives until Bobby turned eighteen if that's what it took to keep him safe.

She reached over and took the pouch out of the drawer beside her bed. She pulled the watch out of the pouch, rubbing her fingers over the etched rose gold. She got up and opened the door, standing in the doorway and looking up at the sky with its bountiful array of stars. The peace of the night surrounded her. She wrapped her fingers around the watch, that somehow always made her feel closer to her mother. "Oh, Mom. I miss you. I know I never even met you, but I do miss you. I wish you were here to know Bobby and we could be a family." She whispered her words into the night air where they drifted slowly away, up to the stars.

Tally sat with Eddie late that night after she'd closed the cafe. She'd propped her feet up on a chair as they sat on the beach under the starlit sky. She was bone-weary tired but couldn't get up the energy to head home and go to bed. So, she just sat.

"It was quite the day, wasn't it?" Eddie's voice broke the silence.

"It was. I'm glad you found Bobby, and he was okay. I'm sure Courtney will give him a good talking to after things settle down a bit. She was so scared when she found out he was missing."

"As any mother would be," Eddie agreed.

"I'm glad he wasn't hurt worse. A few stitches. He'll be good as new soon."

"You know, Bobby said the strangest thing when I found him." Eddie frowned.

"What's that?"

"He said something about Courtney being afraid Kurt would find him."

"Who's Kurt?"

"Bobby wouldn't say, but he told me not to tell Courtney that he said Kurt's name. That he's not supposed to talk about him."

"That's kind of strange." Tally's forehead wrinkled. "I haven't heard her mention that name."

"Well, something is going on with this Kurt fella."

"Maybe I'll get a chance to talk to Courtney about it."

"Might be a good idea."

Tally looked up at the sky and the millions of twinkling lights. "Looks like the weather is going to hold for Julie's wedding. We've had some fabulous days and evenings this spring."

"Yes, it's been fabulous." Eddie smiled at her.

But somehow, she didn't think he was talking about the weather.

CHAPTER 19

E ddie arrived at Magic Cafe precisely at two the next afternoon. Tally had told him she was closing the cafe then and getting everything ready for the wedding. He was going to help whether she'd asked him or not.

"Eddie, what are you doing here?" Tally walked up to him with a big box of vases in her arms.

"I'm here to help." He eyed the vases. "Though I'm pretty sure flower arranging isn't one of my strongest suits."

She laughed that wonderful laugh of hers. The one that made him want to spend every little moment with her. "How about you set the chairs up on the beach? Harry—he's a local, a friend of

Jamie's—he made an arbor for us to use. He just set it up on the beach."

Eddie looked at Tally in confusion.

She laughed again. "Jamie is Susan's son. Harry is Jamie's best friend."

"Got it." *Kinda.* Jamie, Susan, Harry. He repeated the names silently as if that would help keep everyone straight.

"So if you could set up the chairs in rows with an aisle between them, that would help."

"I can do that."

"Great. It's taking longer than I thought to get things set up." She rewarded him with a grateful look.

Eddie headed over to the storage building to rescue the chairs. Outside the building, he ran into Courtney and Bobby. "Hey, Bobby. How you feeling today?"

"I'm good. Momma says I can't go in the ocean for a few days though until my leg heals up."

"That's probably a good idea."

"But I *like* the ocean."

"But you're going to do what your mother says, aren't you?"

"Yeah, I am." Bobby let out an exasperated sigh, one way too large for his small frame. "It's hard being a kid sometimes."

"I bet it is." He nodded gravely as he swiped a hand across his face, choking back a smile.

"Eddie, I wanted to thank you again for finding Bobby." Courtney rested her hand on her son's shoulder. "I'll always be grateful."

"Well, it was more like Stormy found me, but you're welcome. Glad it all worked out okay." He nodded toward the building. "I came to get the chairs. Going to set up for the wedding."

"Can I help?" Bobby jumped up.

"You're supposed to be taking it easy." Courtney eyed him.

"Aw, Momma. I'm fine."

"If it's okay with you, I'll bring him over to where I'm setting up. He can supervise and make sure I set the chairs up *just right*. I promise I won't take my eyes off of him."

"You sure he won't be in the way?"

"Not at all. I'll enjoy the company. Tally said there's a beach wagon in the back of the storage building. I'll pile chairs on that."

"I do need to go get ready. I'm going to help serve at the wedding." Courtney still looked doubtful.

"Go ahead. We'll be fine." Eddie nodded toward the door. "Go."

Courtney headed inside, and Eddie and Bobby went around to the side door to load up the chairs.

"Mr. Eddie?"

"What?"

"Thanks for letting me help."

Eddie smiled at the boy. He'd come to enjoy the boy's company, which in and of itself amazed him. He hadn't really been around kids much. Maybe Bobby was different from most little boys, but Eddie thought the kid was special. Okay, he'd admit, Bobby had him wrapped around his little finger. He loved making the kid happy.

He loaded up the first batch of chairs and they pulled the wagon over to where the ceremony was going to be held. Eddie set up the chairs, and Bobby followed along behind him, commanding him to move the chairs this way and that.

A serious expression crossed Bobby's face, and he frowned and shook his head. "No, move that one this way." Bobby pointed to the left. "And that one, that way."

When they were finished, Eddie gave the setup a critical glance. He didn't want to hurt the boy's feelings, but after he took Bobby back, he was going to have to come back here and straighten some of the chairs. He was pretty sure Tally hadn't meant for him to make a zigzag aisle up to the arbor.

"Come on, Bobby. Let's get you back to your mom."

The small boy looked up at him, smiled, and took Eddie's hand.

He might as well have taken Eddie's heart. A sense of rightness flooded through him. He smiled and Bobby shot him an impish grin. With that, the boy tugged on Eddie's hand and dragged him back down the beach.

Tally looked around the cafe. The dining area was set with white tablecloths and simple flower arrangements on each table. She'd strung white Christmas lights all around the edge of the outside deck and placed thick candles in hurricane lanterns on each table. It was just enough to provide a pretty, festive atmosphere.

Eddie walked up to her. "The chairs are all set. Bobby helped me." He grinned. "But we might want to straighten out a few of the rows. I didn't have the heart to do that after Bobby told me where to set each and every chair."

Tally laughed. "Come on. We'll go straighten them."

They crossed onto the sand, and Tally moved

some chairs around to straighten the rows. She stood back and bit her lip, trying to decide if it was all perfect.

"It looks great, Tally."

"I hope Julie thinks so." She walked up the aisle and adjusted a bunch of flowers intertwined on the arbor. "That's better."

Eddie laughed. "If you say so."

She looked back at him. "I just want everything to be… perfect. Julie has waited a long time to be part of a family. She deserves this. She's the kindest, sweetest, most giving person I know. Reed makes her happy. That's all I want for her."

"Then Reed's a lucky man to have her." Eddie took a step back, looking around. "I think you did a wonderful job pulling off this wedding at Magic Cafe on such short notice."

She *was* kind of proud of how it had all turned out.

"Well, I should be going and let you get ready."

"Oh, Eddie. Julie said you should come to the wedding."

"But…"

"No, really. She knows you're… important… to me. She'd like you to be here. As my guest." Tally paused. "*I'd* like you to be here."

"Well, if both you ladies want me here, I'll be

here. I'll just run back to the inn and change." He turned to leave.

Tally reached out and stopped him. "I really do appreciate all your help."

"Tally, don't you know by now? I'd do anything for you."

Her heart flipped in her chest, and she wanted to answer him. Say *something* after his brave words.

He stood in front of her, waiting for her to say something.

But she didn't. Couldn't.

He slowly turned and walked away.

Tally stood with her mouth open, wondering how she and Eddie had gotten to this point. Again. For a second time in their lives.

But she wasn't really sure she believed it. She knew how quickly things could be taken away, just when you thought all was right with the world.

CHAPTER 20

J ulie stood at the edge of the deck at Magic Cafe and frowned. "Where are the rest of the chairs?"

Tally smiled. "That *is* all the chairs."

"No, really. Where are the rest?" Julie did some quick math in her head, and there was no way there were enough chairs. Maybe this had been too much for Tally to handle. But then, when was anything too much for Tally?

"Here, Reed wanted me to give you this note." Tally reached into her pocket and pulled out a small envelope.

Julie frowned and reached for the note. She slowly opened it and scanned the words.

*My Dearest Almost-Wife,*

*I know you don't like me making decisions without talking them over with you, but please indulge me this one. I've canceled the invitations to all the people except for our good friends here on the island. I know a big wedding was never what you wanted. You were just trying to do what you thought I wanted.*

*All I want is to marry you.*

*Marry you surrounded by the people we love.*

*I hope you're okay with this. I love you very much.*

*Reed*

Julie's eyes filled with tears. "He did this for me? I thought he wanted a big, fancy wedding. The kind he was used to in Seattle."

Tally reached over and hugged Julie. "I think all

he wants is you. Pretty sure he'd be okay if it were just you and him."

Julie looked out over the intimate setup of chairs. It was just perfect. Reed knew what she needed, even when she didn't. Her heart felt like it was going to burst with happiness, with the feeling that all was right in her world.

Julie looked at Tally and let out a long, drawn-out breath. A breath she felt like she'd been holding since the whole wedding planning had begun. "Oh, Tally, I just love him so much."

She smiled. "I know you do. And he loves you. I couldn't be more pleased for both of you." Tally put her arm around Julie's shoulder and they went inside to get Julie ready for her wedding.

Julie stood in front of the mirror, turning back and forth, admiring the vintage dress she'd chosen. She loved the dress they'd finally picked out. The dress had a secret pocket, and when she'd first tried it on, she'd found a note from the woman who had first worn the dress. The note had wished the new owner much happiness on her wedding. She reached her hand into the pocket, fingered the note still there, and smiled, so connected to the Barbara woman who had first worn the dress years ago.

Susan walked up to her. "You look lovely, Julie."

"I feel… well, it's so strange to be all dressed up like this. You did a great job with my hair."

Susan had pulled Julie's hair up into a simple, loose bun with tendrils of hair that framed her face with lacy wisps. Tally came to stand on the other side of Julie.

Julie looked into the mirror, sandwiched in between her dearest friends in the world. Everything was falling into place today. She couldn't be happier.

"You ready to go?" Susan glanced at her watch.

"I am. I'm more than ready."

Julie followed her friends outside, into the lovely warm light of the evening. She took a look down the aisle and saw Reed standing by the arbor.

She started down the aisle seeing the small crowd of faces of her dear friends. Her heart swelled with happiness and contentment. Reed smiled encouragingly as if welcoming her home.

*He was her home.*

He reached out his hand.

She took the last few steps to him and took his hand. He squeezed it and tucked her by his side.

They said their vows to each other, words she would hold in her heart forever.

"You may now kiss the bride."

Reed leaned down and kissed her, then whispered in her ear. "I've waited for this day for a long time."

She looked up into her husband's face, tears trailing down her cheeks. She reached up a hand and touched his face.

"I've waited for this day for my whole life."

Reed pulled Julie aside at the reception, over to the edge of the deck.

"Reed, we have guests we need to talk to. What do you want?"

He leaned down and kissed her. "That."

"Oh, well, then." Julie reached up and wrapped her arms around Reed's neck and kissed him.

A deep chuckle escaped his throat. "I'm going to like this new married gig I have going."

"Me too." Julie sighed and leaned against her new husband.

Reed nodded toward Tally and Eddie on the other side of the room. "So, what's up with those two?"

"I wish I knew. I think Tally likes him. Well, likes him again, I guess it would be. But I'm not sure. I'm not sure that she'll *let* herself care about him." Julie leaned her head against Reed's shoulder. "I wish she would though. I want her to be as happy as I am."

"So I make you happy?" Reed's voice was low against her hair.

"You do. So very, very much."

He turned her around and pulled her back into his arms. "That's all I want. I want for you to be happy."

With his arms firmly around her, she allowed herself to be held and be happy. She and Reed were their own little family now. What she'd always wanted. She let out a sigh of contentment.

Reed murmured against her ear, "I will love you forever."

CHAPTER 21

"I'm so glad you came." Julie smiled up at Eddie. She stood at her husband's side, their hands clasped together.

Eddie didn't think that he'd seen Reed drop Julie's hand all evening. The man looked blissfully happy. The couple was obviously deeply in love, starting out as a married couple, a family.

He hadn't had that in his adult life and hadn't really thought he missed it. But being back here on Belle Island, seeing Tally again... it stirred up all kinds of thoughts that he hadn't had before. Thoughts of settling down. Thoughts of being a couple.

Thoughts of Tally.

*Lots* of thoughts of Tally.

"You having a good time?" Tally stood beside him as if conjured up from his musings.

"I'm having a wonderful time."

"Tally, I couldn't have asked for a nicer wedding. Thank you so much for having it here." Julie smiled.

"It really was great," Reed agreed with his bride.

"Couldn't have been happier to do it." Tally brushed off their thanks, but Eddie could see she was glad they were pleased with how the wedding and reception had turned out.

Julie and Reed wandered off to talk to more of their friends, but Tally stayed at his side, watching the guests mill around. Some stood in small groups laughing, a few couples hung around at the edge of the deck looking out at the starlit sky.

He stayed by Tally's side the rest of the evening, even helping her clean up after all the guests were gone.

Finally, it was just the two of them. Tally looked around the cafe, scanning to see if they'd missed anything.

"It's all good, Tally. Anything else can wait until tomorrow. You look exhausted."

"I am a bit tired." She slipped off her shoes. "And these things are killing me."

"Let's go sit on the beach for a little bit and unwind."

"That's sounds good." She led the way to two lounge chairs near the water's edge.

He sat down and leaned back, watching as Tally relaxed and closed her eyes. And yet, he was determined to disturb her.

"Hey, Tally?"

"Hm." She didn't open her eyes.

"Can we talk for a few minutes?"

She turned to him and opened her eyes. "What about?"

"Can we talk about us?"

"There really is no us, there's just… history."

He sat up and swung his legs between their chairs, taking her hands in his. "There *is* an us. Right now. I know you feel it."

She remained silent.

"Tally, it's taken me a long time to say this to you…" He drew in a deep breath of the salty air. "I love you. I always have. I never quit, not even all those years I was away from here."

"You're just confusing the past with now."

"No, I'm not confused. Not one little bit. I know exactly how I feel." His heart pounded. Oh, his feelings were real. Very real. Cutting to the soul real. "What I want to know, *need* to know, is how *you* feel."

Tally looked down at her hands, then slowly lifted her eyes to look at him. "Eddie... I can't. I don't even deserve your love. I let everyone believe the lie about who Jackson's father was. I never even got to tell Jackson about you. I should have told him all about you. I kept thinking there would be time. I made so many mistakes. But I just can't let myself... I can't feel that way about someone again. I'd never be able to pull myself out of the abyss of losing someone I... uh... *care* about again, so I can't let myself get in that position."

"So you do care about me." Eddie ignored all the excuses she gave.

Tally closed her eyes. "I *can't* care about you, Eddie."

"Open your eyes. Look at me."

Slowly her lashes lifted. The fear he saw in her eyes tore at his heart. He wanted to take that fear away and convince her it would work out. He would be there for her this time.

"I love you. Take a chance with me. We can be a family, you and me."

Tally stood up, looking down at him where he sat on the lounge. "I don't think I can do that. I'm not brave enough. There's a special place in a person's heart for family… and that place is gone for me. I can't care that much… and then lose my family again. I can't."

"You could try." He reached up toward her.

She sidestepped his hand. "I'm not meant to have a family. I lied to my son his whole life, and the universe gave me what I deserved." She shoved her hair away from her face. "You deserve better than me. Someone who will give you their all. Someone who is willing to take risks. Risks like I should have taken all those years ago when you asked me to leave with you. If I had gone with you, Jackson would still be alive. You shouldn't love me, Eddie… you should *despise* me."

Tally spun around and hurried across the beach, back to Magic Cafe.

His heart plummeted. He'd never been able to persuade Tally to change her mind once it was made up.

Ever.

Why had he thought this time would be any different?

The next morning Tally sat in Susan's office, sipping on tea.

181

"So you told him you don't love him?" Susan eyed her with a look of incredulity.

"No... not exactly. But I didn't tell him I loved him either."

"But he said he loved you."

"He... did. But he doesn't mean it. He's just confused with the past. Confused about his feelings after finding out about Jackson. He'll get it all sorted out when he leaves."

Susan cocked her head to one side. "He's not leaving any time soon."

"What are you talking about?" Tally set down her glass. She'd figured after her stern rebuff Eddie would be out of town the next day.

"He just paid for another week's stay at the inn."

"He can't. You can't let him." Panic started to race through Tally.

"And why not?"

"He has to leave. I can't keep seeing him."

"Because if you do, you'll have to admit how you feel about him, admit you love him." Susan raised an eyebrow.

"I *can't* love him." Tally jumped up from her chairs. "I can't risk that. Not again. Besides, I don't deserve him. I kept the truth about him from everyone. Especially from Jackson. He should hate me, not love me."

Susan stood. "Tally, sometime you're going to have to forgive yourself. You did the best you could. You did what you thought was right at the time. If we all had twenty-twenty hindsight, we all might have chosen different paths at some point in our lives. But we live with the choices we made."

"My life is fine, just the way it is." Tally's words sounded defensive, even to her. "I have Magic Cafe, my friends here on Belle Island. I have everything I need."

"Do you? Maybe it's time to take a risk with your heart." Susan walked around her desk and stood by Tally.

"I don't think I can."

"You are braver than you think you are, my friend."

CHAPTER 22

Courtney laughed as Bobby swung a palm frond in an arc above his head. "It's a lightsaber, Momma."

"Of course it is." She laughed again. Bobby could make anything and everything into a complicated game of some sort.

He raced down to the water's edge and back, fighting off imaginary... *somethings*... as he ran. She couldn't remember if he said they were aliens, monsters, or pirates today. She sat on the beach, watching him play. The sun set his blonde curls on fire. He'd tanned up since they'd been here, even though she'd been vigilant with the sunscreen Tally had given her, insisting she had way too many bottles of it around. He looked the picture of a happy, healthy little boy.

If only she could give this to him forever. She looked up and down the beach, always watching, always searching. Then, she leaned back on her arms and let the sun wash over her. She closed her eyes against the glare, letting the warmth soak into her. She sat back up and touched the pocket watch locket she'd put on this morning, wanting to feel that connection with her mother. She wrapped her fist around it while she watched Bobby cavort on the beach. With a sigh, she stood.

"Bobby, come on. Time for me to get ready and you to go to Miss Belinda's."

Bobby dropped the frond and came racing up to her. "Oh, good. Miss Belinda said that we were going to bake cookies today and learn something called frictions."

"I think you mean fractions." Courtney took Bobby's sandy hand. They walked to the door of the storage building. She smiled as they entered the room. A bowl of shells Bobby had collected with Tally sat on a coffee table. Tereza had made curtains from some extra material she said she had sitting around. Susan had brought her two bed tables that she said were extras from the inn. The main room was starting to look like a home.

But it wasn't a home, she had to remind herself. They'd have to move on. Sadness swept through her at the knowledge that all this would soon be a distant memory.

"Bobby, I'm going to go change for work. How about you dump the sand out of those shoes? Get that book Miss Belinda is reading to you and pack up your backpack. I'll be ready to go in a few minutes."

"Okay, Momma. I can't wait. All three guys are gonna be there this afternoon."

She smiled as he sat on the edge of the deck and tugged off his shoes, dumping a beach-full of sand back onto the ground. She hurried inside, grabbed clean clothes, and went into the bathroom to change.

She walked out of the bathroom, about five minutes later, brushing her hair as she walked. "Bobby are you—" She froze.

"Hello there, Courtney." Kurt's voice held more threat than welcome. He stood just inside the doorway with a firm grip on Bobby's shoulder. "You didn't think you could hide forever, did you?"

"Let him go." Courtney lowered the brush, her knuckles white on the handle.

"Ah, Bobby and I were just catching up. Father to son."

"Momma?" Bobby's voice wavered.

Courtney took a step forward. "Kurt, what do you want?"

"What do you think I want? The money you stole from me."

"That was my money."

"Nah, it was *our* money."

Kurt had always thought that anything she earned was his, and anything he earned—which had never been much—was his as well.

"Of course, I also want the kid."

"Momma, I don't want to go with him." Bobby's eyes were wide.

"You're not going anywhere, honey." She took another step closer to Kurt. She had to get Bobby away from him.

Kurt tightened his grip.

"Ow. You're hurting me, Kurt."

"How many times have I told you to call me Dad?" Kurt's voice held a menacing tone.

"I'm sorry…" Tears rolled down Bobby's cheek.

Courtney glanced around the room, seeing nothing to defend herself with. She'd have to divert Kurt's attention. She'd gotten good at that. She could do it again.

"You're not a father to him."

"Of course I am. The courts said so. They also said I have to pay child support."

"I didn't want your money."

"Well, it seems the courts said differently. So, if I have the boy with me, I won't have to pay."

"You're twisting everything around. Besides, you don't want to be saddled with a kid, now do you?" Courtney inched closer.

"Well, I'm not letting you have him. What kinda mother are you, anyway? You were raised by that crazy grandmother of yours."

She refused to take the bait. She had to remain calm. "Okay, Kurt. We'll both go back with you."

Kurt eyed her. "You will?"

"Sure. I think Bobby missed you, anyway." One more small step. She could almost reach out and touch her son.

Bobby started to speak, but she sent him a mom-look. He closed his mouth and stayed silent.

"Oh, look Bobby, your shoe's untied." She crossed the distance quickly and bent down at the same time she hurled the brush across the room toward a mirror. Kurt spun around toward the sound of crashing glass and let go of Bobby's shoulder. Courtney grabbed him and jumped up, pushing her son behind her.

"You lying—"

Kurt reached out for her, and she started to stumble backwards. He grabbed her by both shoulders and shook her. Her brain rattled in her skull. He released her, and she took a few quick steps toward the door, pushing Bobby to her side. She had to get him out the door. Kurt reached out and slapped her across the face. She took another quick step backwards, falling into the doorway, and shoved Bobby out the door.

"Momma." Bobby wailed.

"Run, Bobby. Don't come back. Run."

Bobby spun around and ran out the door. Kurt turned to catch him, but he was already out the door.

Kurt turned back to her. "You're going to pay for that." He reached down and dragged her back into the building and slammed the door behind him.

Tally stood facing Eddie, trying to convince him to leave Magic Cafe. "Go home, Eddie. We have nothing more to talk about." She flung her hands wide, palms up. "Nothing."

"Yes, we do." Eddie stood his ground, his eyes flashing with determination. "Say you'll go out with me one more time. Go out with me tonight. Just this one more time."

"Eddie..." She wavered, but not much. She didn't know which she was more afraid of—Eddie staying, or Eddie leaving. But she'd already told him it wouldn't work out between them. Why would she put both of them through one more night of torture?

She turned when she heard someone call her name.

"Miss Tally, Mr. Eddie." Bobby came racing up to them and threw himself against Eddie. "Hurry. He's going to hurt her. Come save Momma."

Without another word, the boy whirled around and bolted back down the beach. Eddie sprang into the action and sprinted after the boy. Tally stood in shock, her mind ping-ponging between her thoughts about Eddie and Bobby's abrupt interruption. She felt rooted to the spot, unable to shift gears. She told her feet to move, but they wouldn't. She needed to go help. She scrubbed her hand over her face, breaking the lock on her inertia, and hurried after Bobby and Eddie.

"Bobby. I said to run."

Eddie heard Courtney's voice as he bounded up onto the deck of the storage building. He stepped up behind Bobby and put a hand on his shoulder. A quick glance into the room and he saw Courtney sprawled on the floor. There was no missing the unmistakable red swatch across her cheek.

"What's going on?" Eddie stepped through the doorway.

"Stay out of it, mister. It's family business," a man growled.

"You okay, Courtney?"

She was on her side on the floor. "Get Bobby out of here." Her eyes were wide with fear.

"Bobby, come here. Listen to your dad," the man commanded.

"That's Kurt," Bobby whispered. He pressed against Eddie's side.

Kurt started toward Bobby and Eddie, and Courtney grabbed his leg. The man kicked her.

Eddie pushed Bobby behind him and stepped into the room, grabbing the man's collar. "Hey."

Kurt reached out and swung at him, but Eddie easily blocked the punch. The man took a step back, eyeing the situation, then reached down and grabbed Courtney, tugging her to her feet.

"Tell that guy to leave." Kurt wrapped an arm around Courtney's throat.

"Eddie, take Bobby to safety. Please." Courtney begged. "I'll go with you, Kurt. You don't need Bobby."

"Kurt, I'll call you Dad. I promise. Don't hurt Momma." Bobby pleaded.

So, this Kurt was Bobby's father? Eddie looked the man over from head to toe, assessing his opponent.

"Courtney, I'm not leaving you here with him." Eddie's voice was icy cold as he held back his fury, evaluating the situation carefully.

"Come any closer and I'll snap her stupid little neck." Kurt tightened his hold on Courtney and she coughed, both hands reaching up to tug on his arm.

Eddie didn't think the man was strong enough or smart enough to do what he said, but he wasn't taking any chances. "Okay, have it your way. She's nothing to me." He stepped back, leaving a pathway to the door.

Kurt sidled toward the open doorway, loosening his grip on Courtney only enough so she'd walk with him. He sidestepped Eddie with a wide arc around him, keeping his distance.

"Like I said, it's a family matter."

As Kurt stepped through the doorway, Eddie lunged for him, grabbing the arm he had wrapped around Courtney. The girl slid free as Eddie pulled Kurt off balance.

"Go," Eddie urged her.

She took one quick look, grabbed Bobby, and fled out the door.

Kurt recovered his balance and stood facing Eddie.

"I told you that you should stay out of it." Kurt picked up a broom leaning against the wall and held it menacingly in front of him. "You're going to pay for that."

"Didn't anyone ever teach you not to hit women?" Eddie stalled for time as he glanced around for something to defend himself with. Nothing.

"I don't need a lecture from you, old man."

"Seems like you do." Eddie moved to the left.

"Seems like *you* need a lesson." Kurt swung the broom handle and Eddie dodged it, judging the instant that Kurt lost his balance from the power of his swing.

Eddie lunged for Kurt, and they both went crashing to the floor. Kurt came up punching, but Eddie rolled him to his stomach and sat on him, grabbing one arm and pulling it up behind the man's back.

"Sit still or I'll dislocate your arm." Eddie held

one of the man's arms firmly behind his back, with his knee trapping his other arm.

"I'll take it from here." A uniformed man stepped into the room with Tally and Courtney right behind him.

"Luckily, Sheriff Dave was eating at Magic Cafe, so I turned around and got him." Tally sucked in a gulp of air. "Couldn't keep up with you and Bobby, anyway."

The sheriff crossed over, handcuffed Kurt, and dragged him to his feet. "We don't take kindly to hitting women here on Belle Island. You're in a heap of trouble."

"She deserved it. Extorting money from me each month. Child support. Ha. How do I even know the kid is mine?"

"You can tell all that to the judge. Right now you're headed to lockup, and I don't expect you to be out anytime soon, being that you're a credible threat to this young lady."

Courtney stood in the doorway with an angry welt across both cheeks and a red mark on her throat. Eddie crossed to her and gently put a hand on her shoulder. "Are you okay?"

"I've been better." She smiled wryly, winced, and grabbed her side.

"You should get those ribs checked out. That was a pretty hefty kick."

"Don't I know it."

The sheriff put a hand on Kurt's shoulder and started walking him out the door.

"I'll get even with you," Kurt growled at Courtney.

Eddie stepped in between Kurt and Courtney. "Son, I think you should be careful of those threats. If you ever, ever put a hand on her or on Bobby, you'll be dealing with me. Understand?"

The sheriff led Kurt away, and Courtney sagged against the doorframe. "Tereza has Bobby back at the cafe. I need to go see him and make sure he's okay."

"Come on, then." Eddie put an arm around Courtney's shoulder and he and Tally walked her back to Magic Cafe.

CHAPTER 23

Tereza let go of Bobby's hand as soon as the boy saw them a few yards away on the beach. He went racing across the sand and flung himself into Courtney's arms. Courtney wrapped her arms around the boy.

Tally didn't miss the girl's gasp as he squeezed her tight. "You okay?"

"She probably has a cracked rib." Eddie stood behind her.

"Momma, Mr. Eddie saved you."

Courtney nodded as she brushed the curls away from Bobby's face. "He did."

"He's awfully good at saving people." Bobby let go of his mom and went and wrapped his arms around Eddie's waist. "Thank you, Mr. Eddie."

Eddie looked down in surprise, then lowered himself to look directly at Bobby. "You're welcome, Bobby."

"You don't ever let the bad guys win, do you, Mr. Eddie?"

"I, uh… well, I guess not."

"Kurt *hit-ted* Momma all the time."

Anger swelled through Tally. No wonder the girl was so skittish. She was hiding out from a monster. Courtney started to stand up and grabbed her side. Tally reached down to help her to her feet. Tally looked at Courtney's face with two angry welts across her cheeks. Rage and disbelief flooded through her, along with an overwhelming urge to protect the girl. "Courtney, come with me. Let's get some ice on your face. We'll get your ribs checked out, too."

Courtney nodded and leaned on Tally as they slowly climbed the steps to the cafe. She settled Courtney into a chair, took a good look at her, then turned to Eddie. "Why don't you take Bobby into the kitchen. I bet he could use some ice cream. Bring back some ice in a bowl for Courtney, too."

Eddie nodded and took Bobby's hand. "Come on Bobby, let's get ice cream for your mom, what do you say?"

Tally sat down next to Courtney. "That's why you've moved around so much? Trying to hide from Kurt?"

"Yes. He's Bobby's father... but... he's cruel. At first, it was just aimed at me. But then he got this court order to pay child support, and he got so angry. Then he hit Bobby. He hit his *own son*. I left that night. He found me though, a few days later. I was just at a friend's house. That night he... well, when he was finished, I could barely move for days. He didn't even apologize like he did the first few times he'd hit me. Now it was all my fault because I'd filed for child support and taken Bobby away. Honestly, I didn't even want money from him. I just wanted him to leave us alone. But the state got involved and Kurt said he was going to file for custody and I couldn't let that happen." Courtney's face paled, and she shifted in the chair, holding her side.

"Take your time." Tally's heart was breaking for all this girl had gone through—and she'd gone through it alone.

"I left the next day. I didn't have much. A bit of savings. We packed a few suitcases, and I drove as far away from there as I could." Courtney reached a hand up and gingerly touched her face. "I thought

Kurt had given up on us after a few months, but somehow he located where we were living. We just managed to get away before he got to us."

"Well, we're going to see about making sure Kurt never harms you or Bobby again. There's going to be no more running for you two. I've got a lawyer I'll call in the morning and we'll see what we can do."

The girl's eyes filled with tears. "You've been so good to me, so good to Bobby. I don't know what I would have done if Eddie hadn't shown up. I..." Tears streamed down her face.

"That's okay. You cry if you need to. You've had quite the day."

Tally gathered Courtney into her arms while the girl sobbed.

Eddie peeked out the kitchen door and saw Courtney wiping tears from her face. Tally must have said something that made her smile, though, because the corners of her mouth turned up, but then she winced. Eddie would like to get his hands on Kurt and teach him a lesson or two about how he should treat women. Or better yet, send him so far away that Courtney and Bobby never had to deal with him again.

Tally saw him looking out the door and waved him over. She must have said what needed to be said to Courtney.

"Come on, Bobby. I think your mom would like some of that."

"She loves ice cream." Bobby carefully grabbed the bowl of ice cream and carried it over to his mother.

"Here, Momma. I made it myself. Well, I didn't make the ice cream, but I made the bowl of it. Mr. Eddie let me scoop it out myself. The ice cream was hard. Did you know if you put it in the microwave just a tiny bit it softens so you can scoop it out?" Bobby sat down, breathless, and placed the bowl in front of his mother.

"Good to know." Courtney smiled at the boy.

"Momma, is Kurt gone now? For good?"

"He is if I have anything to say about it." Tally leaned forward and took Bobby's hand. "You were very brave to come get help."

"I was brave, wasn't I?" Bobby swung his feet as he perched on the chair. He turned toward his mom. "Momma, are you going to be okay? Your face looks funny."

"I'll be fine."

"Remember when I took you to the doctor to have your leg checked out?" Tally leaned forward toward the boy.

"Yep. I got stitches."

"Well, your mom needs to see the doctor, too. Her ribs hurt a bit. I'm going to take her and get her checked out."

Bobby shrugged. "Well, at least you won't need stitches." His face was grave. "They hurt even though I said they didn't."

"You were very brave about them," Courtney assured her son.

"Hm. I guess I'm just a brave kid, huh?"

Tally smiled. "I guess you are." Tally stood. "How about I take your mom to get checked out? You stay and finish up the ice cream. Eddie, can you watch him?"

"I can. Bobby and I will go clean up the mess at the storage building, too."

"I don't know…" Courtney looked unwilling to go without Bobby.

"He'll be fine with Eddie. Let's get you fixed up."

Courtney rose slowly from her chair, leaning on the table to steady herself. "Bobby, be good for Mr. Eddie."

"I will, Momma. You be brave at the doctor's."

"I'll try to be as brave as you were."

Bobby puffed up his chest. "Well, you can *try*."

CHAPTER 24

Eddie and Tally closed the door of the storage building behind them after getting Courtney and Eddie settled in for the night. Tally had made Courtney promise to call if she needed anything, but Eddie wasn't sure the girl would bother anyone even if she needed help. He figured both Bobby and Courtney would be out as soon as their heads hit the pillow. Bobby from the excitement of the day, and Courtney from the mild pain pill she'd finally accepted from the doctor.

"I hope I can get her some legal help," Tally said as they trudged back to Magic Cafe.

"She needs a protection order."

"She needs more than that. She needs him permanently out of her life."

"What are you thinking?" Eddie eyed Tally.

"I'm thinking maybe I could talk him into relinquishing his parental rights. It's not like a court is going to give him visitation after all this violence. Maybe then he'd leave them alone. If Courtney decides to stay here… well, she'd do just fine raising Bobby here."

Tally seemed to be able to fix things for everyone she cared about… except for herself.

Eddie reached out and caught her arm. "About that one last talk?"

Tally stopped and looked at him, the moonlight illuminating her face. "I know what you want, but I can't. I have nothing to give. See how quickly things can change? Look what almost happened to Courtney. Her life, Bobby's life… they could have been ruined."

"Everything's a chance in life, Tally. You have to take risks to grab that happiness." He held out his hand. "Tally, I'm offering you that. Happiness. Love. Sharing our lives. All you have to do is reach out and take my hand. We'll face everything together."

Every fiber in Tally's body was screaming at her to take Eddie's hand. Risk it, take a chance. But though her heart said to take his hand, her head said to run away.

Finally, her head won out.

"Eddie, I'm sorry. I know you want me to say that I'll try… but it's just too late for us."

"It's never too late."

Tally looked into his steel blue eyes, memorizing every detail of his face to hold in her memory. She knew how to do that. Tuck a memory away, deep in the recesses of her brain. What she didn't know how to do was to simply reach out and take that outstretched hand. She didn't deserve it. Didn't deserve Eddie.

She missed the chance to tell Jackson about his father. He'd died not knowing the truth. She'd lied to her son his whole life.

Why would she think she deserved happiness after the sins of her past?

*She didn't.* When she loved someone, really loved them, she lost them. It was her destiny.

She balled her hands into fists at her side. "Goodbye, Eddie. I wish only the best for you."

A heaviness settled on her, making her heart ache and her head pound. She turned and trudged away from him. Away from all he offered her. Away from the man who said he loved her.

She walked toward her old, normal life. She was fine with that. She was.

## CHAPTER 25

Julie waved to Susan and Tally, then gave them a just-a-minute sign and ducked back into the kitchen. "Nancy, I'm going to pop out and visit with Tally and Susan for a few minutes. You got things in here?" Of course, her other baker had things under control. She'd run The Sweet Shoppe while Julie and Reed had taken a quick honeymoon.

The honeymoon had been wonderful, but she was glad to be back here in her shop. She'd actually missed it, which was kind of crazy, but it was the truth.

Nancy looked up from where she was rolling out a pie crust. "Sure do. You take a break. You've been going nonstop since you got back. I told you that you should have taken more time."

Julie grinned. Sometimes Nancy was like a mother hen with her. She took off her apron and hurried out to visit with her friends, carrying a plate of chocolate eclairs.

Susan eyed the plate of sweets. "You know, one of us should have opened a salad shop, or a gym, or *something*. I feel like I put on five pounds every time I walk in here."

"I live to serve." Julie grinned and slipped into a chair. She looked over at Tally. "You doing okay? Susan told me Eddie left. I really thought he'd stay around for a while."

Susan glared at Tally. "This woman sent the man packing."

"Tally. Why? He seems so nice."

"It was the right thing to do." Tally's words held a don't-ask-anymore-questions tone.

But Julie couldn't let it go. "I wish you'd just try, Tally. I want you to be happy."

"I'm happy. What more can a woman want? I have a great business, great friends, live on the best island." Tally's words sounded hollow, like she was trying too hard to convince them—or herself.

"Julie's right, you know." Susan reached for an eclair. She took a bite and sent Julie a look of delight. "These are the best ever, Julie."

"Reed signed us up for a cooking class on our

honeymoon. The resort chef made these. I tweaked the recipe a bit, but aren't they great?"

"That Reed is a keeper. Only he would think of choosing a cooking class on your honeymoon. The man knows the way to your heart."

"He does." Julie smiled. Susan turned to talking about her mother-in-law, Mary, and the antics of Stormy. Tally smiled at the appropriate times and answered simple questions, but it was like a light had gone out in her friend's soul. Julie's heart ached for her friend, but for the life of her, she couldn't think of any way to make things better.

Tally was going to have to choose to reach for happiness. Goodness knows, Tally had told her the same thing when she'd been afraid to love Reed and trust him. And look at how that had turned out. They were married and ridiculously happy.

But when Tally made her mind up, there was usually no chance of changing it.

Bobby sat at a table at Magic Cafe, swinging his legs and slowly eating his ice cream. Tally had gotten used to having him around. He'd started hanging out with her when the restaurant wasn't busy. She was glad to give Courtney a break, and the boy always made her smile with his enthusiasm for life.

She plopped into the chair across from him. "Enjoying the ice cream?"

"You have the *bestest* ice cream ever." Bobby scooped up another bite, then set his spoon down. "Miss Tally, can I ask you something?"

"Of course."

"Why did Mr. Eddie leave? I miss him. He's been gone forever."

It had actually only been a week, but Tally understood Bobby's feelings exactly. It did seem like it had been forever.

"He had to go back home, back to work and the life he has there."

"But, I thought he liked us."

"He does. He likes you a whole lot," Tally reassured him.

"He likes you, too. I can tell these things, you know. I'm not a little kid." Bobby picked up the spoon and took another bite.

"He… well, you're right. He does… like… me. But things are complicated."

"That's what grownups always say." He let out one of his huge sighs. "I don't think it's complicated. Do you like him?"

"I do, but—"

"Don't say it's complicated again," Bobby warned. "If he likes you and you like him why doesn't he stay here? He's good at playing space guys, you know."

Tally figured that was high praise coming from Bobby.

"Sometimes grownups just can't be together." She didn't have any idea how to explain it to Bobby.

He set down his spoon again and looked straight into her eyes. "'Cause you're afraid?"

"I..." What could she say to that? Bobby had nailed it.

"Sometimes you have to do things that scare you. That's what my momma says. She says you have to be brave." Bobby jumped up. "My momma is brave, she took me away from Kurt. And Mr. Eddie is brave, he saved me and he saved Momma. I'm brave... I got stitches." He sat back down. "So, you should be brave, too."

Tally looked at Bobby as he finished his ice cream. The boy who was wise beyond his years.

The boy who was braver than she'd ever be.

But maybe the boy was right...

Courtney looked everywhere. She opened her tote

bag and dumped the contents on the bed, carefully sorting through everything. She opened the drawers to the bed table and searched every square inch of them.

She finally dropped to her knees, crawling around the floor, and looked under the beds. Her heart clenched in her chest. She could not have lost it. It was her only connection to her mother that she had left.

Despair flowed through her. She had to find it. She pushed up off the floor and glanced around the room, not knowing where else to look, hoping the pocket watch would call to her and give her a clue where it was. She closed her eyes, willing her mind to tell her where she'd last seen the locket.

Her eyes flew open. She'd had it on the day that Kurt was here. Had it fallen off in their scuffles? Had he taken it?

A chunk of her heart broke off, a missing piece that had always connected her to her mother.

She sank onto the bed and lowered her head onto her hands.

Tally took Bobby back to the storage building after he finished his ice cream. They really should call it something else if it was going to be Courtney's and Bobby's home for a while. Storage building just wouldn't do.

"Hey, we should name your new home." Tally looked down Bobby, their hands swinging back and forth as they walked. "What should we name it? Most of the houses and cottages here on Belle Island have names."

"I get to name it?" Bobby's eyes shone with excitement.

"You sure do."

"Hm… I think I'll name it…" He stood in front of the building, carefully taking in every detail. "I think I'll name it Happy House."

Tally grinned. "That's a perfect name."

"I think so." Bobby went rushing inside of the newly named building.

"Momma, guess what. Miss Tally said I could name this building and guess what we're gonna call it?"

Courtney looked up, and Tally could see she was upset, but she put on a smile for her son. "What are we going to call it?"

"Happy House." He jumped up and down. "Isn't that a great name?"

"It sure is."

"You okay, Courtney?" Tally frowned.

"I… yes, I'm okay. I just lost something."

"What is it?"

"A lady's pocket watch on a chain. My mom had it. It's all I have of hers."

Tally's heart thundered in her chest. She'd had a lady's pocket watch of her mother's also. It had been her grandmother's before that. But it was lost now, too. She'd given it to Jackson, and she'd never found it after he was gone. Maybe he'd had it with him when their boat went down. He said he often slipped it into his pocket for luck.

"Momma." Bobby went over and hugged his mother. "Don't be sad. I know where it is."

"You do?"

"I found it under that table over there. I put it in my treasure chest. I knew you'd be sad if you lost it. But… I forgot about it. I'm sorry."

He jumped up and raced over to his treasure chest and came back, triumphantly holding the watch in his hands. "Here it is. See, Momma? Now you don't have to be sad."

Courtney's eyes filled with tears. "Oh, Bobby. Thank you."

"Don't cry. I gave it to you so you'd be *happy*, like Happy House. I know you like this necklace thing. It doesn't even work though."

"I know it doesn't, but it means a lot to me."

A painful twinge of disappointment overcame Tally. She knew exactly how the girl felt. She herself had always felt connected to her mother when she held the watch. "May I see it?"

Courtney held the watch out to Tally. She carefully held it in her hand, letting the thick gold chain slip over her fingers. She briefly closed her eyes, lost in her own memories, then opened them and examined the watch.

She turned it over and gasped at the words engraved on it. Her breath caught, then she let it out ever so slowly. She traced a finger over the engraved surface.

"This was your mom's?"

"Yes. I found it in her things. She had a memory box of sorts. I took this with me and a photograph. That's all I have of her."

Tally clutched the watch to her chest. "This… this is my grandmother's watch. The one my mother gave to me… the one I gave to my son."

Courtney jumped off the bed. "Are you sure?"

"Yes, I know the inscription." *You'll always be my Belle.* Tally touched the locket in awe. "My grandfather gave this to my grandmother on their wedding day."

"But why did my mother have your watch?" Courtney frowned.

Tally's heart thundered in her chest. "Come with me." She hurried out of the storage building—Happy House—and over to Magic Cafe with Courtney and Bobby hurrying behind her.

She led them into her office and sat at her desk. She yanked open a drawer and slid out the photographs Eddie had found in Jackson's notebook.

"Do you know her?" Tally showed the photo to Courtney.

The girl gasped. "That's my mother. I've seen that photo before. My grandmother showed it to me. My grandmother said that boy in the photo was to blame for my mother dying."

"What? My Jackson would never hurt anyone."

"That was just my grandmother's strange way of putting things. My mom died in childbirth when she had me."

"I'm sorry."

"I miss her even though I never knew her. That's silly, isn't it?" Courtney's face held a wistful expression, then her eyes widened. "Do you think…" She stared at the photo. "Tally, do you think your son, Jackson, is my father?"

"I… I'm not sure." Tally's hand shook as she set down the photo.

"I think the reason I was so drawn to Belle

Island is because of that inscription. I just know when I saw the sign to here that I turned and came over the bridge. It was like the island was calling to me. Do you think that's strange?" Courtney's forehead wrinkled.

"No, I think… I think it was meant to be." Tally stared at the watch.

"He must have given this watch to my mom…" Courtney picked up the photo. "They look happy, don't they?"

"Very happy." Tally almost couldn't get the words out. Emotions race through her. She looked at Bobby standing beside Courtney, unusually quiet while the grownups talked. She wanted to reach out and touch him, could he possibly be…

"You know… the only other thing I have is in this velvet pouch where my mom kept the watch. It's just a note with a bunch of words and letters on it, but I can't make any sense out of it."

Tally's heart thundered in her chest. "Some words and random letters?"

"Yes. I've kept it, but I don't know what it is."

"Can I see it?"

Courtney took the pouch out of her pocket and carefully opened it, took out the worn, folded note, and handed it to Tally.

Her hand shook as she reached out for the note,

not daring to breathe, not daring to believe. She carefully unfolded the note and spread it flat on her desk, her pulse pounding in her temples.

There it was.

In Jackson's handwriting.

Written in the secret code they'd devised so many years ago. A secret code just between mother and son.

*And evidently shared with Courtney's mother.*

Tally grabbed a piece of paper and pen and started to translate the note, frowning a few times as she struggled to remember some of the quirks of the code. When she finished, she sat and stared at her translation.

Courtney came and stood behind her and read the note out loud over her shoulder. "Kim, I'm going to tell my mother and grandfather about you and the baby when I get to Belle Island. I'll be back for you as soon as I can. Wait for me. All my love. Jackson."

Courtney gasped.

Tally's heart turned over and emotions flooded through her. Jackson had planned on telling her but then had died at sea before he had a chance. She wondered if he'd told her father before they died. Had his last thoughts been about Kim and the baby?

"That would mean that…" Courtney stared at Tally. "That would mean that I'm your granddaughter and Bobby is your great-grandson."

Tally's hand flew to her heart. She looked at the boy with the one dimple on his left cheek. Just like Jackson. "That *is* what it would mean," Tally whispered. She turned to Courtney. "And I've got more news for you."

"What else could you possibly have to tell me? More than this?" Tears threatened to spill from Courtney's eyes, and her voice shook.

Tally reached out and took Courtney's hand. *Her granddaughter's hand.* "I'm going to tell you who your grandfather is, too."

CHAPTER 26

E ddie unlocked his door and stepped inside after a long, lonely walk. He'd wanted the peace and quiet of no interruptions, so he'd left his phone in the apartment. Though, why he wanted that was beyond him. All he'd done was think about Tally. An interruption would have been a welcome relief.

He picked up his phone now, hoping to distract himself from the thought that dogged him. There were two missed calls, three text messages, and an email notification.

All from Tally.

Part of him wanted to just delete them without listening or reading… but he couldn't quite get up the nerve to do that. He wanted to hear her voice.

He tapped the phone and listened to the phone message—every tone of her voice made him aware that something was up. A tension flowed through her words and an unmistakable edge haunted her request to *please* call her.

Maybe she'd changed her mind about him? A flicker of hope threaded through him followed quickly by a dull sense of foreboding.

Or was something wrong back on Belle Island? Was Kurt back messing with Courtney and Bobby?

He glanced at his watch. If he jumped in the car now, he could be there in Belle Island by sunset. He'd rather hear what she had to say in person.

Or maybe it was just an excuse to see her again, have a chance to convince her...

He grabbed his overnight bag and was on the road within ten minutes.

Courtney sat at a table at Magic Cafe, sipped on a sweet tea, and waited for Tereza to finish her shift. She had to talk to her friend before she exploded from the weight of all that had happened today. Her emotions raced along a roller coaster and refused to let her get off the ride.

Tereza plopped down in the chair across from

Courtney with a big glass of ice water in her hand. "I just clocked out. You look… flustered. Or something. What did you want to talk about?"

"I don't even know where to start." Courtney set down her glass. "So much has happened."

"I just saw you this morning."

"My whole life has changed since then."

"Okay, kind of melodramatic, but I think you better start explaining." Tereza eyed her.

"I'm bursting to tell someone."

"I'm your girl. Spill it." She leaned forward.

"You're never going to believe this. I'm… I'm Tally's granddaughter.

"What?" Tereza sat up straight. "But, I thought… I've heard rumors… I mean, her son has been gone for years."

"Her son, Jackson, was my father. We just figured it out." Courtney mindlessly dumped some more sugar into her tea… and she didn't even like her tea sweetened.

"I don't even know what to say."

"Me either. We figured it out because of this." Courtney wrapped her hand around the watch hanging around her neck.

"Wait, one thing at a time. So, you and Tally and Bobby. You're all just one big family?"

"It gets better. You know, Eddie?"

"Yep." Tereza cocked her head to one side. "Tally's friend."

"Well, it ends up that Eddie was Jackson's father."

Tereza gulped a big swallow of water. "So you, like, have… an instant family all of a sudden? Wow, I can't imagine having a better grandmother than Tally."

"I can't either. She's certainly different from my mom's mother. My grandmother on my mother's side couldn't have cared less about me. She was a cold, hard woman." Courtney was dazed from all the day's revelations. "I don't even know what to think. But I'm so happy that Bobby has a family. A real family. Tally has already been so good to us, but now… Bobby is over the moon."

"How's Tally doing? That's a lot to take in during one morning." Tereza took another long swallow of ice water.

"I *think* she's happy. She seemed happy. Well, and shocked. Just like I am."

"But you found out your father is dead now, didn't you?" Tereza reached out and squeezed Courtney's hand.

"I did, and it's sad. But I've always had this empty place in my heart regarding my father. I knew nothing about him. I at least will be able to find out things about him now. What he was like."

"It seems like such a huge coincidence that you ended up here on the island." Tereza's forehead wrinkled.

"It was all because of this watch. It has an inscription in it that says 'you'll always be my Belle.'" Courtney clutched the watch hanging from her neck. "I'd seen it when I was a young girl, but I'd forgotten about it. The back used to open easily, then it got stuck, and I was always afraid to pry it open, afraid I'd break it. Tally got it open and knew it was her watch that she'd given to her son. I think when I saw the sign to Belle Island, somewhere deep in my subconscious, I remembered that inscription."

Tereza smiled. "I think that sometimes the universe conspires to bring us right to the place we're meant to be."

"Maybe you're right." Courtney nodded. She looked out at the ocean, stretching before her. Tally and Bobby were down at the beach, collecting shells. For the first time in her entire life, she felt like she was home.

Tally paced back and forth across the beach in front of Magic Cafe. She glanced at her phone in her hand. Why hadn't Eddie called her back? She considered leaving another message, but how many did it take?

Maybe he wasn't going to call at all. Maybe he was that angry with her. But she needed to tell him the news.

He was a grandfather.

He had a granddaughter and a great-grandson.

This time he'd know the truth. He'd be able to spend time with Courtney and Bobby. Everyone would know about Eddie being Jackson's father. They'd know the truth. The whole truth.

*Even the truth that she loved him.*

If he would ever talk to her…

She sank onto a lounge chair and watched as Bobby chased the waves, his favorite pastime. Her granddaughter sat by the water's edge, watching her son. Her family, right within her view. Something she never thought she'd have again, but now she'd never give it up in a million years.

"Tally?"

She jumped at the sound of Eddie's voice and looked up, her heart swelling with joy at the sight of him.

Eddie was oblivious to her swirling emotions and stood with his hands in his pockets. "You left some messages for me. I thought I'd come see what is so urgent."

Tally sprang up and went to Eddie. "Oh, Eddie, you came."

"So what's the reason you were blowing up my phone?" Eddie's voice sounded cautious, and she couldn't blame him.

"Here, sit down. I have something to tell you."

"I'll stand." He eyed her with a bit of defiance.

"Okay, but you'll wish you'd sat down."

He crossed his arms and stared at her.

"I have news... about Jackson."

Eddie narrowed his eyes. "What about him?"

"He... Oh, Eddie, he had a daughter." Tally felt a smile spread across her face, spread across her very soul, and happiness flooded through her.

"He what? How do you know? How did you find out?"

"It's a long story involving a lady's pocket watch and a secret code. But let me tell you the best part first."

"Which is?"

She reached out and slipped her hand in his. He looked down at their hands and for a moment she was afraid he was going to pull away, not that she could blame him. She reached her other hand up to touch his face and he covered her hand, giving her hope. He might have missed his son growing up, but she was filled with the joy of giving him a family now. A chance to watch Bobby grow. She suddenly knew, she was *certain*, she'd do anything for this man.

She caught her breath and nodded down toward the shoreline. "See Courtney and Bobby down there by the water?"

Tally watched as Eddie swiveled his head to look at the duo at the shore.

"Those two. They are your family. She's your granddaughter, and he's your great-grandson."

Eddie slowly sank down on the lounge chair, his face a mask of surprise.

Tally grinned. "I told you that you should sit."

"But, how? I mean… what?" Eddie raked a hand through his hair. "How did you figure all this out?"

"Like I said, it's a long story, and I'll explain it all, but it's all true. I'm sure of it." Tally touched Eddie's shoulder, but what she really wanted to do was hug him with all the exuberance she felt rushing through her.

Bobby looked up and let out a whoop. "Hey,

Mr. Eddie is here." The boy came racing across the beach and threw himself at Eddie. "You came back. Did you hear the news? We're a family." Bobby jumped up and whirled around.

"I… yes…" A dazed expression covered Eddie's face.

Courtney slowly walked up to them, one arm wrapped around her side. She still hadn't recovered from her bruised ribs. "Hey, Eddie." Her voice was tentative.

Eddie rose and took a step closer to Courtney. They stood looking at each other, then Eddie opened his arms and Courtney walked right into his embrace.

Right that minute, with Eddie hugging his granddaughter, and Bobby dancing around them, all was right in Tally's world.

*Almost* everything.

Tally stood at Lighthouse Point with Eddie. The sun drifted toward the horizon, throwing splendid shades of orange and purple into the fluffy clouds. A salty breeze drifted around them.

"It was quite some day, wasn't it?" Tally stood by Eddie's side.

"It was. I never thought… Well, I couldn't be happier." He looked out at the ocean.

"Eddie, another thing. You know how you wanted to have one more talk with me?"

"Yes?"

"If we could have it now? I mean…" Tally touched his arm and he turned toward her. She looked right into his amazing blue eyes. "I love you, Eddie. I always have. It might be too late now. I know I sent you away. But… I want to try. I want to be with you. I want us all to be a family." She looked down at the water sliding over her feet. "I admit I'm scared, but I know it's what I want."

Eddie tilted her head up to look at him. "I've waited forever to hear those words from you. To hear you say you love me."

"I do love you, Eddie."

He leaned down and kissed her gently. "I love you, too."

She touched his cheek and bathed in the warmth of his smile.

Eddie's eyes were filled with wonder. "You know how you told me you made a wish here at Lighthouse Point that you'd get your family back? Wishes do come true at Lighthouse Point. We didn't get our son back, but we did get our family."

A peace that Tally hadn't felt in so many years

washed over her like a gentle, cleansing wave. "That we did."

He wrapped an arm around her shoulder as they watched the sun slip below the horizon in one final burst of light.

CHAPTER 27

Tally ran her hand down the cream linen on her wedding suit. She looked in the mirror at her reflection, hoping that Eddie wouldn't only see the older woman she'd become, but look inside at the girl who had been so in love with him all those years ago. She'd waited a long time for this day.

Courtney walked up behind her. "You look lovely."

"Thank you. I feel… well, it all feels a bit unreal to me."

Courtney hugged her. "Everything is all so new for all of us, isn't it? Bobby is beside himself, bragging to everyone about his Pops."

"Eddie loves that Bobby calls him that." Tally was pretty pleased with being called Grams herself. So much had changed in the last few weeks. Eddie had moved to the island. They'd pulled off this wedding in record time. Eddie had insisted that he'd waited years for this. No more waiting. She smiled as she thought of his persistence. Not that she didn't want the very same thing. Once she'd made up her mind to marry him, she wanted to be his wife without any delay.

"It's so strange to have a real family now." Courtney smoothed the skirt of her blue floral bridesmaid dress. She was wearing the rose gold pocket watch on a chain around her neck. Tally had gotten the watch fixed for her, and it now kept perfect time.

Tally glanced at Courtney's simple blue flats. "Good to see you in new shoes, too." She grinned at the girl. *Her granddaughter.* Sometimes she felt like she needed to pinch herself to make sure all this was real.

"Hey, I also bought a new pair of sneakers when I got these. I figure now that I don't have to save money to run away, I could at least get comfortable shoes to wear while I work."

"Good plan. I couldn't be happier about you

and Bobby staying here on the island." Tally looked back in the mirror. What would Eddie see when he looked up and saw her walking toward him?

Susan popped into the room. "The best man sent me in and told me to tell Momma and Grams to hurry up."

Julie hurried into the room, too. "You look fabulous."

Tally looked at her two friends. "You know, we've all come such a long way in the last year. Julie, you found Reed. Susan found Adam, and I'm back with Eddie." Her heart swelled with happiness and gratitude. Her blessings were many.

"We are very lucky." Susan smiled. "Not to mention you have a family now."

"I do." Tally squeezed Courtney's hand.

"So are you ready?" Julie asked.

"I'm ready." Tally took one last look at her reflection, and for the briefest moment, a girl of eighteen stared back at her and nodded encouragement. Then, all she saw was herself, now. Older, and hopefully much wiser.

"Let's go." Tally and Courtney stepped out of Happy House and into the sunshine. The wedding ceremony was out on the beach, with chairs lining the aisle. Susan and Julie had tied bows on the chairs and made two simple floral arrangements up by the arbor. Every detail was perfect.

Courtney walked up the aisle and stood waiting for Tally. Eddie and Bobby stood at the arbor. Eddie's eyes shone with happiness and he grinned at her.

She felt a smile spread across her face. With confident strides, she floated down the aisle to this man she'd loved her entire life. This man and her family. All standing together.

They said the vows they had prepared, and the minister told Eddie he could kiss his bride.

"Hey, Pops, you gonna kiss Grams or what? I think that makes it legal or something," Bobby piped up.

Everyone laughed, and Eddie did as their great-grandson said. He leaned over and kissed her ever so gently on the lips. Then with a whoop, Eddie scooped her up and twirled her around like they were young kids again.

All of their friends stood up and clapped. Tally looked over at Julie and Susan and smiled at them. Her friends had tears in their eyes.

She'd never been happier or felt more complete.

"I love you, Tally." Eddie bent down and whispered in her ear. "I always have, and I always will."

Now she had tears in her own eyes.

"Courtney, Bobby, come with us." Eddie held out his arms and the four of them, a family, walked down the aisle together.

THANK YOU for reading my story. I hope you enjoyed it. Sign up for my newsletter to be updated with information on new releases, promotions, and give-aways. The signup is at my website, kaycorrell.com.

Reviews help other readers find new books. I always appreciate when my readers take time to leave an honest review.

I love to hear from my readers. Feel free to contact me at authorcontact@kaycorrell.com

**COMFORT CROSSING ~ THE SERIES**

The Shop on Main - Book One

The Memory Box - Book Two

The Christmas Cottage - A Holiday Novella (Book 2.5)

The Letter - Book Three

The Christmas Scarf - A Holiday Novella (Book 3.5)

The Magnolia Cafe - Book Four

The Unexpected Wedding - Book Five

The Wedding in the Grove (crossover short story between series - Josephine and Paul from The Letter.)

**LIGHTHOUSE POINT ~ THE SERIES**

Wish Upon a Shell - Book One

Wedding on the Beach - Book Two

Love at the Lighthouse - Book Three

Cottage near the Point - Book Four

Return to the Island - Book Five

**INDIGO BAY** ~ a multi-author series of sweet romance

Sweet Sunrise - Book Three

Sweet Holiday Memories - A short holiday story

Sweet Starlight - Book Nine

Made in the USA
Middletown, DE
13 March 2019